The Lost

Hellhounds Series: Book 7

Theo Mann

Invisible Publishing Company

Hellhounds Series

Contents

Chapter 1

Captain Owen LeMaine rotated his cannon downward and fired directly into the bunker roof, only to take a face full of lasers in return. The enemy onslaught smashed the Hunter-class fighter craft *Belligerent* in the nose.

Corporal Elliot Monk veered the helm hard to the left to avoid more cannon fire erupting from the ground under the ship. The *Belligerent* angled away into the atmosphere, but she still took plenty of lasers on her belly as she retreated.

"These bastards don't want to give up!" Monk yelled through the communications system.

"We'll just have to teach them," LeMaine yelled back. "Bring her back around from the north. Galo, you come at them from the south. We'll split them up and flatten them that way."

"Acknowledged," the reply came from an Imoliv fighter craft swerving around the bunker's other side.

The *Belligerent* swung back to face the bunker and the Imoliv dropped into position across the planet Zukion's rolling fields.

The Imoliv pilot nodded to Monk and LeMaine through his cockpit window. The Imoliv team that had been working with the Hellhounds during the war against the Axichis was ready to rock and roll.

Galo steered the helm while his brother Lutov manned the fighter's forward cannon. Two more cannons on the ship's sides showed where Sindra and Tavon sat ready to pound the Axichis into oblivion.

The combined Elian and Imoliv alliance had driven all the Axichis spacecraft out of the Elian system. The Axichis didn't threaten Elia anymore.

Now the Elian Military had to hunt down the last Axichis holdouts scattered throughout the solar system. Most of them had barricaded themselves into bunkers like this one.

The Axichis survivors fought tooth and nail to hold their positions. The alternative was death.

Galo swooped in low and his team bombarded the Axichis cannons. The lasers pivoted in his direction and Monk made his move.

He gunned the engines and the *Belligerent* plunged out of the atmosphere. She streaked in low while the Axichis cannons were pointed the other way.

LeMaine nailed his gunfire into the cannons and all the Hellhounds opened up at the same time. The laser cannons exploded under the Hellhounds' combined fire and the blast knocked both ships out of the way.

Monk fought to stabilize the ship. By the time he got her straightened up, the *Belligerent* hovered in exactly the same place where she started, but no more laser fire came from the bunker.

"Eat some of that, shitheads!" Corporal Molly Nunn called from the back. "That will teach you to invade our system!"

"Keep it together, Hellhounds," Lieutenant Stuart Peterman replied from his cannon placement. "We still have to get down there and finish off any survivors."

"And you know what that means," Sergeant Brien O'Hara added. "It means they'll try to resist."

"I love it when they resist," Corporal Glenn Heckler growled. "It's so cute when they think they actually have a chance."

"Lock and load, Hellhounds," LeMaine ordered. "We're going down."

He gestured for Monk to lower the *Belligerent* to the ground and the Imoliv fighter copied her. The Hunter and the Imoliv set down on either side of the destroyed laser cannons.

"Imoliv move in," LeMaine ordered. "Monk and Galo, stay on board and cover us from up here."

"Yes, Sir," Galo replied.

LeMaine hopped out of his seat and climbed into the *Belligerent's* rear compartment. The Hellhounds stood around waiting for him by the open hatch. He signaled them to deploy and they all shouldered their carbines.

The squad separated outside the hatch, surrounded the *Belligerent*, and trained their weapons on the cannons, but nothing moved over there.

The cannons lay in pieces with the bunker roof blasted open. The squad swept the area, but they didn't find anything.

LeMaine pointed to Sindra, Lutov, and Tavon and signaled west. Sindra nodded and took his team that way while LeMaine and the Hellhounds headed east. They found the hidden bunker entrance hidden in a stand of trees a hundred yards away.

The Elian Military had been exposing enough of these hidden Axichis bunkers on nearly every Elian planet. The Hellhounds knew the drill by now, which meant Axichis pilots and soldiers would be waiting underground to shoot anyone who broke into their bunker.

LeMaine stuck his carbine through the door leading to the stairs. Everything sounded quiet down there. He tiptoed down the stairs and halted at another reinforced door several floors below the surface.

He nodded to Nunn and she knelt down, tore open her pack, and primed her Plaostine charges. She gathered her Plaostine blocks in her hands and nodded back to LeMaine, who nodded to the Hellhounds opposite him.

Lieutenant Polasek took Heckler, O'Hara, and Sergeant Krista Lemon on his side. Peterman and Sergeant Mason Kellogg scooted in behind LeMaine. All the Hellhounds held their breath and braced themselves for the assault.

LeMaine stepped away from the wall, positioned himself right in front of the door, and fired his carbine into the lock. It blasted off its hinges and he barely ducked out of the way before a million lasers exploded from inside. One grazed his shoulder as he dove clear just in time.

Nunn pitched three Plaostine blocks through the opening, one in each direction and one straight ahead. The Hellhounds covered their heads and a deafening boom rocked the bunker as all the charges detonated.

Dust and smoke erupted from the doorway and all the Hellhounds charged inside firing into the smoke. Lasers flickered from both sides, but that only showed the Hellhounds where the Axichis were hiding.

The Imoliv team burst in from the opposite stairway and surprised the Axichis from behind. All the Axichis had been facing the Hellhounds and fell to the Imoliv team's fire.

The two teams split up in pairs to search the rest of the bunker. It had been set up exactly the same way all the other holdout bunkers had been. This top floor acted as a control room with electronic equipment, communications arrays, and stacks of extra supplies.

LeMaine and Polasek worked their way to the right while the other Hellhounds attacked and finished off the Axichis taking cover behind their supplies. LeMaine didn't see anyone over by the controls, which was lucky for everyone involved.

LeMaine and Polasek halted by the control station and looked down at it. "It looks like everything is still working," LeMaine remarked.

"They've been in contact with their own system within the last solar cycle, I'd say," Polasek agreed.

"That's perfect. Come on. Let's go downstairs and see what we can find."

LeMaine left the Hellhounds to guard the upper floor while he and Polasek crossed to a different door. It opened into a third, internal stairway leading to the bunker's lower levels.

The two men descended to a second story beneath the control room. Seven shiny new Axichis fighter craft sat parked there.

"They're brand, spanking new," Polasek observed. "None of them has a scratch on them. The Axichis definitely haven't flown these ships during the war. The Axichis must have been holding these fighters in reserve for something else."

"Just like everything else in these bunkers. They were definitely planning a second wave after they conquered the planet."

"Or maybe they just liked making extra contingency plans. Maybe they just planned for the worst and left these ships and supplies to cover their asses."

"It doesn't matter. We have a job to do." LeMaine waved Polasek toward the fighters. "Take your pick and make sure it's fit to fly. We gotta get going."

Polasek grinned with delight on his way to the nearest Axichis fighter. That guy got way too excited when it came to machines.

LeMaine went back upstairs and found Heckler, Lutov, and Lemon holding three Axichis at gunpoint. Most of them were bleeding and the Hellhounds had pushed them down on their knees between stacks of crates.

"What's the story?" LeMaine asked Heckler.

"They don't know nothing," Heckler growled. "They're playing stupid...because they are." He hit one of the Axichis across the back of the head.

"That isn't likely to improve his memory, Heckler," Peterman pointed out.

LeMaine stepped in front of the Axichis prisoners. Two of them glared at him. The other wouldn't look at him at all.

"You contacted your command in your own system within the last day," LeMaine began. "What were you communicating with them about? Are the Axichis coordinating another campaign to invade Elian space?"

"How would we know?" the Axichis on the far left muttered.

"Why did you communicate with them, then, jackass?" Lemon snapped.

"We were trying to find a way home, of course," the second one replied. "We were trying to find a way to get across the border into our own system without getting attacked by the Elians."

The first one shot LeMaine another death glare. "Kill us and get it over with."

"No, I'm not going to kill you."

"Torture, then?" The Axichis squared his shoulders and straightened up. "We can handle torture."

"I'm not going to kill you or torture you," LeMaine replied. "I'm going to give you your wish. I'm going to take you home."

All three Axichis snapped their heads up to stare at LeMaine, but he only turned away. The conversation was over.

"Get them out of here," he told the Hellhounds, "and don't lay another finger on them. We need them in perfect health for the journey. After you get them squared away, all of you suit up and get ready to drop. We're going behind enemy lines."

Chapter 2

L eMaine followed the Hellhounds, who marched their three Axichis prisoners downstairs at gunpoint. The Hellhounds had shackled the prisoners hand and foot and chained them together so they couldn't move a muscle except to talk.

Monk, Heckler, Kellogg, and Sindra shoved the prisoners on board the Axichis fighter craft that Polasek had chosen. The Hellhounds steered the prisoners to a compartment right behind the cockpit.

Polasek sat at the controls and he didn't look up as the squad passed him. Kellogg went over to him and checked the scanners. "The prisoners' life signs are all reading as normal. They're ready to fly."

LeMaine wedged himself into the compartment where Heckler and Sindra knelt on the floor shackling the prisoners' ankles together. Now they really wouldn't be able to move.

"If you stay in here and don't move or cause any trouble," LeMaine told the prisoners, I might see my way to letting you go when we get back to Axichis space."

"You're a liar," the first prisoner snarled. "You'll kill us to stop us from telling anyone you're infiltrating our space."

"Your race pretended to be our friends and then invaded our system," LeMaine replied. "Don't tempt me."

He walked out and watched from the corridor while the other Hellhounds left the compartment. They locked the prisoners in and everyone returned to the cockpit. The Hellhounds had to cram in shoulder to shoulder just to fit.

Sindra worked his way nearer to the controls and fitted a small device to the fighter's bulkhead. He switched it on.

"It's working," Peterman announced. "It's masking our life signs. The fighter is reading with three Axichis on board and no one else."

"Excellent," LeMaine replied. "Take us out, Monk, and step on it. I don't want to stand around in this tin can any longer than I have to."

"Yes, Sir." Monk stepped forward and Polasek left the pilot's station to let Monk sit down.

He fired up the engines, released a trigger on his controls, and the bunker's launch bay slid back. Blue sky opened above the fighter. The *Belligerent* and the Imoliv team's fighter craft had already departed. The Hellhounds were on their own.

Monk slammed the throttle down and the fighter rocketed into the air at full speed. It burned through the atmosphere, plunged into space, and took off at a wicked pace heading for the Axichis border.

The instant it left orbit, dozens of Elian fighter craft and bombers launched from all over Zukion, closed around the fighter, and bombarded it with cannon fire.

Pounding smashes rocked the ship. LeMaine flattened himself against the bulkhead and cringed with every strike. "Return fire, Monk!" LeMaine ordered.

"I *am* returning fire!" Monk hollered.

"They certainly are enjoying themselves!" Peterman called.

LeMaine winced again as another punishing blow slapped the fighter off course. The Elian Military hounded the fighter across the system to make it look like they were trying to stop the fighter from escaping.

The bombers could have destroyed the fighter easily, but the next second, Monk pulled a wild, looping diversion, dodged several more cannon shots, and streaked across the border into Axichis space.

Axichis warships launched from several planets. They all rushed to the border, but the Elian bombers pulled up there and didn't cross.

"Keep it going, Monk!" LeMaine yelled. "Execute our strategy."

Monk didn't turn around. He yanked the helm hard in one direction and then another. At the same instant, the left engine burst into flame the way Polasek had programmed it to.

The ship veered wildly out of control. Monk didn't have to pretend to fight the helm. He leaned all the way back in his chair and his muscular arms strained to the limit holding the ship on course.

"Now, Lieutenant!" Monk bellowed over his shoulder.

Polasek tapped the remote on his wrist and the right engine exploded. The fighter plummeted and Monk barely managed to stop it from crashing in ruins on a planet inside Axichis space.

The left engine held out just long enough for Monk to pull the nose up level with the ground. The ship's momentum kept it going and it crashed into a forest. Branches and leaves whipped past the cockpit window and then the ship flew nose first into a tree trunk.

Everyone in the cockpit hurtled forward and landed on top of Monk and the controls. Groans and bellows of protest drifted out of the pile before everyone peeled themselves out of the confusion.

LeMaine hauled himself upright and checked his remote. "We're there. We're fifteen miles from the city. That was perfect, Monk."

"Just don't ever do it again," Kellogg added.

"Do you think I wanted to do it this time?" Monk countered. "Blame the captain. This wasn't my idea."

"Arm up, Hellhounds," LeMaine ordered. "Let's get out of here and make sure the area is secure. Polasek, get on your array and make sure none of the Axichis are coming around to check on us."

"What do you want to do about our three friends?" Lemon asked.

"Bring them out here," LeMaine replied.

Heckler and Lemon went into the back to get the prisoners. Polasek set up his array. "No one is coming. The warships are all standing off against the Elians across the border. They don't have time for us."

"Good." LeMaine turned to the corridor, but Heckler and Lemon still didn't come out with the prisoners.

LeMaine strode down there and found the two Hellhounds bending over the three Axichis. "What's the problem?" LeMaine asked.

"They're dead," Lemon murmured. "It looks like they used some kind of suicide drug."

Heckler stood up and moved out of the way so LeMaine could see. The three Axichis lay on the floor with their eyes closed. They looked like they were asleep.

"Get Kellogg back here," LeMaine told Lemon.

She left and returned with Kellogg a second later. He examined the prisoners, but he couldn't do anything about this. They were all dead.

"What do you want to do, Captain?" Heckler growled.

"This could work in our favor," LeMaine replied. "We don't have to worry about these three telling anyone what they know. Unshackle them and bring the bodies up to the cockpit."

LeMaine went forward and ordered everyone outside. Then he ordered Nunn to lay Plaostine charges around the fighter's hull.

Heckler and Lemon positioned the Axichis bodies in the cockpit seats and the Hellhounds retreated to a safe distance before Nunn blew what was left of the fighter craft.

"Now we'll have to find another way off this planet," Sindra observed.

"That was our plan to begin with," Peterman replied.

"Let's move out, people," LeMaine ordered. "We need to get as far away from the wreck as we can before someone comes around snooping."

The squad hiked into the mountains following their remotes to the nearest city. LeMaine pulled up on a wooded hilltop and observed the metropolis through his binoculars. "The strategic center is on the far eastern edge of town. We can get near it under cover and then make our strike."

"What are we striking?" O'Hara asked.

"Everything," LeMaine replied. "Communications arrays, ships, command posts—any high-value asset. We'll know more when we get closer."

At his word, several Axichis fighter craft and warships soared down through the atmosphere and landed at the strategic center he'd just been observing.

"That proves it," he went on. "The same ships that threatened the Elian border came from here. We need to hit them hard and fast and then disappear into the woods."

"They'll know we're here as soon as we make our first strike," Polasek pointed out.

"That's why we need to work fast. Let's go."

The squad kept moving for the rest of the day. At sundown, they came to a halt on another hill east of the city.

From here, LeMaine could see every detail of the strategic center. A large airfield covered most of a broad area south of the communications array. Dozens of dishes pointed at the sky.

"They're all pointed at Elia," Peterman observed. "That isn't good."

"None of this is good," Heckler growled. "Look at all those ships. They're as new as the ones we found in the bunker. These assholes are planning something big."

"That's why we're here—to stop them," LeMaine replied. "They have cannons. That's perfect."

"How is that perfect?" Lemon asked. "Those cannons are bigger than anything we've seen yet. They're big enough and powerful enough to hit any vessel inside Elian space."

"It's perfect because we won't have to look too far to find a weapon big enough to destroy all those ships. We can use the cannons to wipe out the array, too. We just need to figure out a way to get inside the compound."

The moment he said that, a bunch of vehicles buzzed over the landscape approaching the strategic center from the city.

The vehicles looked like larger-than-average Axichis fighter craft except that these didn't fly through the air. They hovered just off the ground and skimmed the surface.

"They must be carrying freight," Polasek suggested. "They're too big to be anything else."

The craft approached the strategic center's outer perimeter, went through a checkpoint, and the sentries on guard waved the vehicles inside.

LeMaine kept an eye on them, and a little while later, the same vehicles skimmed out the same way and headed back to the city.

"Let's go," he ordered and the Hellhounds set off down the mountain.

They came to the same route and LeMaine gave orders to the Hellhounds to shelter on either side of the vehicles' flight path. Nunn laid a charge in the very center where the vehicles would be certain to fly over it.

The Hellhounds concealed themselves just as another group of vehicles came along following the same route. This was almost too perfect.

Nunn blew her charge right under the lead vehicle and all the others came to a stop. Their pilots dismounted and approached the stricken vessel to discuss the damage.

LeMaine circled his forefinger over his head and the Hellhounds darted out of hiding. They crept up behind the very last vehicle, clambered on board while the pilots' backs were turned, and hid among the cargo.

The pilots must have been under orders to consult with someone if anything went wrong. They didn't start flying again for a long time, but when they did, they flew straight into the compound with no trouble. The sentries didn't even search the freight craft.

Now came the tricky part. The vehicles pulled up at a warehouse where another crew unloaded the cargo. LeMaine didn't see how the squad could get away unseen, but he got lucky again.

The vehicles had to stand in line while the crew unloaded one after another. The last vehicle with the squad on board had to stand there unattended. The wait gave the Hellhounds all the time they needed to jump off and sneak away into the compound.

They regrouped behind a different warehouse. "We gotta find the cannons," LeMaine whispered to the others. "This way."

The squad raced from one building to another, ducked and hid to let more sentries pass, and darted to the next concealed spot before anyone saw them.

LeMaine crouched behind a building and observed the cannons not far away. They covered an entire field and Lemon was right. These guns were much bigger.

These didn't have a capsule to house the gunner. Instead, an entire control room perched at the end of each gun where the gunner sat. The control room walls concealed the person inside, so the walls must provide the display to show the gunner whatever they were shooting at.

"How do we get out there without being seen?" Polasek asked.

LeMaine jerked his thumb over his shoulder. "See if you can hack your array into one of the cannon controls."

"And then what?" Polasek asked.

LeMaine grinned at him. "Have fun with it. As soon as you make your move, we'll make ours."

Polasek smirked, crawled backward into the compound, and vanished among the buildings.

"How long is this likely to take?" Lemon muttered.

"Not as long as it would take for us to go out there and take those cannons by force," Kellogg pointed out.

"If they catch us, they could turn the cannons on Elia," Peterman added. "We need to remove all the cannons at one stroke."

"What do you think Polasek is going to be able to do with just one little array?" O'Hara asked. "He might not even be able to......"

An ear-splitting crash cut him off. All those enormous cannons had been sitting idle with their giant muzzles pointed at the same area of the sky.

Now, one of them wheeled sharply to the left, hummed downward, and opened fire on the line of cannons directly next to it. A gargantuan laser fired from its barrel and torched thirty cannons in one shot.

All those guns exploded in a catastrophic series of booms that shook the planet. The Hellhounds ducked under their arms. "Holy shit!!" O'Hara shrieked. "Don't screw with Polasek!"

"Take cover!" LeMaine roared as another cannon farther down the line opened fire.

This one sat in a position fifteen guns down from the original cannon that took out half the field. The second gun erupted to its right, demolished all the remaining guns on that side, and left fifteen cannons intact at the center of the field.

As soon as only these fifteen remained, they all went haywire at once. Four rotated sideways and unloaded on the airfield dotted with thousands of ships. The cannon swiveled in wild sweeps cutting all those ships down in a ground-shaking series of explosions going off one after another.

Three more cannons turned on the compound itself. They rotated this way and that devastating everything in their path. They imploded buildings, brought vehicles to the ground, sliced sentries in half, and tore the fence to shreds.

The Hellhounds crouched in place, not daring to move. The cannons kept wheeling and rotating in all directions shooting everything as far as the eye could see.

Several warships launched from the far end of the airfield where the cannons hadn't been able to destroy them yet. They streaked across the landscape toward the compound, but the center grouping of cannons never moved. They stayed where they were with their barrels pointed to the skies.

The warships flew right into their path and the guns erupted, spat massive lasers into the sky, and detonated those warships to clouds of dust and burning fuel.

The cannons reduced the whole strategic center to rubble in a matter of minutes. LeMaine didn't even see Polasek or where or how he did it. This one was going down in Hellhounds history.

Noise and flying debris ripped through the compound in exploding hurricanes. The Hellhounds couldn't move. Axichis troops ran for cover only to get blown up in their own buildings or to fall to more cannon fire gunning them down.

The bombardment kept up for at least fifteen minutes. The cannons stayed active until they blew up every warship that dared to come within range.

After a while, the cannons fell silent, but distant explosions kept going off across the wasteland where the compound had been. LeMaine raised his head and looked around. The compound had been utterly leveled, just like that—all except for the one building where the Hellhounds had been hiding.

"I take back every insult I've ever made against Polasek," O'Hara murmured. "He's the biggest badass on the block—bigger than you, Heckler. Sorry, but that guy is a flippin' monster."

"You got that right," Heckler muttered. "I'll never give him a hard time again."

"You might want to save your promises for later," Peterman replied. "Here he comes."

A small, slight figure appeared out of the haze. LeMaine got to his feet as Polasek strode over to the squad with his array tucked under his arm.

He smiled at everyone and then grinned at LeMaine. "You told me to have fun with it, so I did."

LeMaine clapped him on the shoulder. "I'm glad you enjoyed yourself. You did real good."

"We should get out of here," Peterman remarked. "We don't want any Axichis to read us on their scans."

"You're right," LeMaine replied. "Let's fall back."

The Hellhounds turned away, but before they could leave, Polasek jumped. "Oh, wait! There's one more thing I have to do."

"What is it?" Nunn asked.

Polasek pulled out his array, set it on the ground, and tapped on it. The last remaining cannons purred around in circles, aimed at each other, and they all fired at the same time.

All the cannons exploded in towering columns of flame. There was nothing left.

Polasek stood up and shut his array. "Now we can go."

Chapter 3

The Hellhounds retreated into the mountains. "Where are we falling back to, Captain?" Kellogg asked.

"We need Polasek to pick out our next target," LeMaine checked the sky. "We won't be able to travel there before dark. We need to select a rendezvous point in case we get separated. I don't want to use that crashed fighter. It's too obvious."

"There's an abandoned ruin on that hilltop over there." Polasek pointed out the hill in question and then showed it to LeMaine on his remote. "There are no Axichis life signs around. We can meet there and it's easily visible from any direction."

"That will work." LeMaine synchronized his remote to the rest of the squad so they could all find the location if they needed to.

Polasek took out his array again. "There's another strategic center on the other side of the city. It will take too long to go around. We need to find a way to get through town without being seen."

"That's impossible, Polasek," Monk pointed out. "We're Elians with four Imoliv. Everyone will recognize us."

"That's why I said we need to do it without being seen," Polasek replied.

"What do you suggest?" LeMaine asked.

Polasek squinted at the countryside. "Those vehicles that came out to the compound were carrying all kinds of supplies including weapons."

"How do you know that?" Nunn asked.

"Didn't you look to see what they were unloading at the warehouses?" Polasek asked. "The Axichis had crates of laser rifles all over the place."

The Hellhounds exchanged glances, but no one replied. LeMaine had to admit that he hadn't been looking at the supplies then, either. Leave it to Polasek to notice a detail like that.

"I say we pull another ambush on the next convoy that comes out here," Polasek went on. "Only this time, we should take out the whole party without damaging the vehicles at all. We need to knock out the drivers, commandeer the vehicles, and then take the convoys back into town as though we're on our return trip. We can get into town and cross to the next strategic center without anyone noticing."

"How do you plan to take out the whole convoy without damaging the vehicles?" Nunn asked. "We won't be able to use Plaostine."

"No, we won't, but there's another way we can do it," Polasek replied. "Those vehicles had different markings. The ones carrying weapons had specific markings that were different from the ones carrying fighter craft fuel, food, and medical supplies." He looked up at LeMaine. "It's just an idea."

LeMaine waved toward the Hellhounds. "Take over. I'm all ears."

"Well, it's simple, really. We need to create a diversion that brings the convoy to a halt. Then we sneak on board the vehicle carrying weapons and steal their rifles. They're easier for pinpoint targeting."

"How can we pinpoint-target the drivers if we're already on board their vehicles?" Heckler countered.

"Oh, come on, guys. Use your heads," Polasek fired back. "The drivers will stop at the wrecked compound. They'll have to talk to each other to decide what to do, now that they can't deliver their cargo. We'll slip off the vehicles, take cover in hidden locations, and use the laser rifles to take out the drivers. Then the vehicles will be ours without a scratch on them. Oh, come on! I can't be the only one who thinks of this stuff."

"How do we divert the convoy to stop without blowing up one of the vehicles?" Galo asked.

"Nunn can set off a charge like she did before," Polasek replied. "This time, instead of blowing the lead vehicle, she can set it off right in front of the lead vehicle. All the drivers would have been warned about the last time. They'll be on the lookout and they'll come to a stop."

Peterman clapped him on the back. "You're the man, Polasek."

"He certainly is," LeMaine replied. "Let's get into position before the convoy shows up. Nunn, lay your charge."

The squad got to work and hunkered down on either side of the supply route just as the next convoy of vehicles hummed into view. The whole operation went exactly as Polasek predicted.

Nunn blew her charge in front of the lead vehicle. The convoy came to a stop while the drivers got out to discuss the situation and to report it over their communications equipment.

The Hellhounds darted out of hiding and concealed themselves on the vehicle Polasek said was carrying laser rifles.

He pointed at one of the many crates in the back. As soon as the vehicle started moving again, Monk pried open the crate and handed out laser rifles to all the Hellhounds.

LeMaine peeked out when the vehicle came to a halt again. The drivers stopped outside the burned wreckage of the former compound. They held another lengthy conversation and called in to report that, too.

They took way too long deciding what to do. They left the Hellhounds plenty of time to jump out of the vehicle and gun down every driver before any of the Axichis personnel even realized they were in danger. None of them was even armed.

"Load up and turn these things around!" LeMaine called to his squad. "Get back on the road before they figure out the original drivers are gone."

He scrambled into the driving compartment of the nearest vehicle. It didn't have any windows. An electronic display covered the inner compartment wall so he could see where he was going.

"This is perfect," Polasek exclaimed through the intercom from the next vehicle. "No one will see us like this."

"Where are we going, Polasek?" Kellogg asked. "We can't just drive these into the next installation."

"No, we can't, but the good news is we have enough weapons now. We shouldn't have any trouble taking down that one, too."

"You direct us, Lieutenant," LeMaine told him. "Tell us where to go."

"Fall in convoy behind me," Polasek ordered. "Everybody stick together. Don't break the convoy no matter what. We need to convince everyone that we're still working together."

He took off across the countryside. The controls on LeMaine's vehicle showed the route back to the city and the warehouse these vehicles came from.

Polasek followed that route exactly—right up until the moment when he drove straight past the warehouse. He kept on going deeper and deeper into the Axichis city.

The vehicles steered themselves following the vehicle in front of them. Only Polasek needed to keep track of where they were.

That left LeMaine free to study the Axichis city. It looked oddly familiar apart from all the people being Axichis instead of Elian.

Then LeMaine figured out why it looked familiar. The Axichis had adopted Elian technology here, too. The architecture resembled Elian architecture. The layout of cities and buildings didn't differ that much from what he might have seen on any Elian planet.

In fact, Elia had more diversity between planets. Some were far more exotic than the Axichis society. Why would the Axichis take such an interest in conquering Elia if the Axichis went to so much trouble to copy Elian society?

Polasek's voice brought LeMaine back to his senses. "We're coming up on the strategic center. We still have four hours of daylight left. Do you want to make a play for it now or wait until tomorrow?"

"If we don't go for it today, we should keep on driving," Peterman suggested. "We can camp somewhere outside the city and come back into town on this side after sunrise."

LeMaine checked their position on the vehicle's controls. "Let's make a play for it. What's the plan, Polasek?"

"Can you hack it with your array again, Polasek?" Sindra asked.

"That probably isn't such a great idea," Polasek replied. "The Axichis will be expecting it. We need to come up with something different. I say we drive these vehicles as close to the compound as we can. That way, we'll have all these supplies on hand to use against the......"

A devastating crash cut him off. LeMaine scrambled to see anything from inside this vehicle. He had to fumble with the controls before he realized the awful truth.

The lead vehicle in the Hellhounds' convoy, the vehicle that Polasek had been driving, sat right in the middle of the street, its driving compartment blown to a ragged inferno. The vehicle sat dead and still in the middle of the road.

"Polasek!!" Peterman yelled through the intercom. "POLASEK!!"

No one answered. The vehicle had been completely destroyed.

Kellogg sprang out of the vehicle behind LeMaine's and charged Polasek's vehicle. Kellogg made it twenty feet away when, out of nowhere, a howling shriek plummeted from the clear blue sky.

A projectile of some kind dropped on the vehicle Kellogg had just exited and the vehicle detonated in flames. "We're under assault!" LeMaine roared. "Pull out and scatter! Get as far out of town as you can! Separate! Don't stick together! Meet back at the rendezvous point!"

He seized his controls and ripped his vehicle away. He should have been paying more attention to where Polasek had been leading them and how to drive this thing.

LeMaine careened through the streets without watching where he was going. He only cared about putting as much distance between himself and the other Hellhounds as possible.

He also tried to steer away from the strategic center Polasek had been planning for the squad to hit. Something must have triggered an alarm when the vehicles didn't return to their warehouse.

Another missile slammed into the street right in front of him. He yanked the steering mechanism hard to the side and skidded into an alley, but it wasn't big enough for the vehicle.

It scraped the walls on both sides and would have gotten hopelessly wedged between two buildings. He dragged it up and gunned the throttle for all he was worth.

He rocketed over the roofs and gulped when he spotted five Axichis fighter craft closing in on him. Now the whole Axichis force knew the Hellhounds were on this planet.

His first instinct told him to shoot at the fighter craft, but this vehicle didn't have any weaponry. He was defenseless except for the laser rifle on the seat next to him.

He had to ditch this vehicle. It was too obvious.

He veered away from the fighter craft and plunged back down onto the streets. He swerved onto a footpath, knocked people and other vehicles out of the way, and wreaked havoc everywhere he went. The Axichis only had to follow the trail of chaos in his wake.

He didn't care anymore about where he stopped. He had to do it now. It was the only way he could disappear.

He slammed the helm sideways, skidded around a corner, pulled the vehicle to a stop, and sprang out. He was still wearing his backpack and he only paused long enough to snatch his rifle.

He bolted into another alley, clambered over a wall, ran down another street, and hid in a different alley to catch his breath. The fighter craft tilted overhead searching the vehicle and the surrounding streets.

LeMaine was hardly less visible now. He couldn't let anyone see him. Every man, woman, and child on this planet would recognize an Elian and turn him over to the authorities.

He needed to conceal his identity, but that would be difficult with Axichis civilians walking all over the place. He had to wait for night to fall and then get out of the city at all costs.

Chapter 4

LeMaine shrank away when armed Axichis soldiers trooped through the streets outside the alley where he crouched to hide himself. He couldn't go out there without someone seeing him.

He backed away to the end of the alley, climbed another wall, and made his way through a few back streets only to nearly run into another Axichis patrol. They were searching the whole neighborhood for him. He couldn't stay out in the open like this.

He darted into a dark doorway to hide, but a few minutes later, the Axichis came down the alley searching for him here, too.

He retreated even farther, and when he could still hear their voices, he pulled open a random door, climbed some stairs to the second floor, and watched them from an upstairs window.

They strode up and down the alley talking and pointing their rifles into every corner. He flattened himself behind his window hardly daring to breathe until they left.

He collapsed there commanding his brain to think. He needed to come up with some way to get out of here unseen.

He turned away and studied the building in which he found himself. This level appeared to be deserted and abandoned.

It didn't contain any interior walls or furniture. A thick layer of dust covered the floor and some of the upper windows had been broken out. The building looked so different from the rest of this cosmopolitan city.

He explored deeper into the building trying to find a way out, but he still planned to come back to this abandoned floor until dark. This would be a perfect hiding place.

He opened another door leading into a dim hallway. He almost went back the way he came, but then he heard the noise of machinery and vehicles coming and going. The sound came from behind him—from the other side of the building.

He followed the hallway, inched through another door, and found himself on an upper mezzanine overlooking some kind of factory. Enormous machines chugged away on one side of the lower floor with technicians working around them.

More freight vehicles drove into the warehouse, parked, took on cargo, and drove back out into the city. They gave LeMaine the same idea of stowing away on board one of them. Maybe they would take him out of town or at least away from the areas where the soldiers were looking for him.

He crept down the mezzanine looking for a way to get down there without being seen. The mezzanine wrapped around the lower warehouse and he turned a corner to position himself directly above the incoming vehicles.

He searched the factory again, and for the first time, he spotted a glassed-in chemical lab on the opposite side. It had been underneath him when he first entered the factory. He didn't see it before.

Masked and suited lab techs worked on their equipment in there. LeMaine couldn't see what they were doing except that they were working some kind of machinery, too.

The machines stamped down and left tiny vials of some nameless fluid on the next conveyer belt beneath them. These vials passed through a few more machines that packed and loaded them into crates.

Mechanical transport robots trucked the crates out to the vehicles. This factory must be mass-producing whatever substance the Axichis were making in that lab.

LeMaine didn't think anything of it. He started to turn back to study the incoming and outgoing vehicles when he whipped around fast.

He froze and his blood ran cold when he saw a man enter the lab and step up to the technicians' workbench. The man wasn't Axichis. He was human and he definitely did NOT belong to the Hellhounds.

LeMaine's heart stopped when the technicians surrounded him, pulled up the sleeve of his short-sleeved shirt, and injected something into his upper arm. The man stood numb and impassive through the procedure and then walked out of the lab the same way he walked into it.

LeMaine couldn't blink. He couldn't move or breathe. He watched in stunned horror as a different man stepped into the first guy's place and the Axichis injected him with something, too.

A line of human males followed, each one cooperating with the procedure. None of them offered any resistance. They stared straight in front of them with the same blank, dull, brainless expression. Their eyes never flickered from one side to another. There was no one home at all.

LeMaine swallowed hard. This couldn't be happening. What were all these humans doing here—inside Axichis space? He didn't have to wonder. The Axichis were experimenting on them with whatever substance these chemists were producing in their lab.

LeMaine glanced back at the vehicles coming and going. He was running out of time before night fell. If he hoped to catch one of these vehicles out of the warehouse, he had to do it now.

His curiosity and horror wouldn't let him. He had to find out what the Axichis were doing with these captive humans.

No doubt remained in his mind that the Axichis must have captured these people. Did they capture these humans during the war and bring them back to Axichis space?

LeMaine would have heard about that. The Elian Military Command never would have tolerated it. Command would have mounted a massive campaign to get these people back. Outrage would have spread through the Elian system. Everyone would have known about it.

No one knew about this. How did the Axichis capture these men without anyone realizing what they were up to? He couldn't figure it out, but he had to. He was the only Elian alive who knew about this.

He either needed to find a way to free these men or take the news back to Elia. He would find out what the Axichis were doing, beat it back to the rendezvous point, and scrub the whole mission.

Weakening the Axichis and stopping another invasion wasn't nearly as important as getting word back to Command about this. The whole Elian population needed to know about this.

Invading Elia meant nothing compared to this. Elia and the Imoliv had the frequencies. They could stop the Axichis from invading again.

This experiment gave LeMaine a really bad feeling. The Axichis could have been conducting these experiments for decades, all while pretending to be Elia's allies.

That thought gave LeMaine the chills. These men could have come from anywhere. They could have been civilians kidnapped from any Elian colony or planet.

The Axichis had been trading inside Elia all these years. They could have snatched random people here and there—never enough to spark anyone's concerns. The thought staggered LeMaine's mind.

He checked his remote and discovered more human males in the basement levels of this building—a lot of human males. At least fifty of them occupied a level beneath this one.

The line leaving the lab followed another set of stairs to the lower level, but LeMaine couldn't see those stairs from here.

He snuck down back down the mezzanine and hunted around until he found a way to get past the walls. He found another stairway leading downward.

He checked every floor in the building. Almost all of them were deserted except for the factory, warehouse, and loading area. They opened into an alley away from the street where no one would see what the Axichis were up to.

He descended even farther. Three floors below street level were also deserted, but he struck pay dirt when he got to the fourth floor. He glanced through a doorway and had to shut it immediately when he saw a vast gymnasium-style cavern beyond.

He also spotted another stairway on the other side of the building. All the men from the lab used that stairway to get down here where they reentered the gymnasium.

LeMaine retraced his steps and used his remote to find the stairs. A continuous line of men came down them to the gymnasium.

LeMaine opened a random door and blundered into the stairway before he realized it was even there, but none of the men even looked at him. They kept marching down, down, down in their zombie trance.

His skin crawled just standing this close to them. Their eyes registered not the smallest wink of recognition or intelligence. The Axichis had completely wiped these guys out and left their bodies walking around perfectly healthy.

They were all powerfully built, muscular, and their skin shone with health. The Axichis maintained these men in the peak of physical condition....for what?

LeMaine didn't want to know, but he had to find out. He couldn't leave this building without getting to the truth.

He joined them until they entered the gymnasium where he got his answer. They all started training and fighting each other with different weapons, wrestling, shooting Axichis laser rifles, and lifting weights.

These men could lift unbelievable loads, and when they threw each other, the impact shook the floor. Some of them even fired weapons at each other, but their bodies didn't take damage the way normal human bodies did.

They didn't do this with laser rifles, of course. They definitely would have taken damage from those.

No, they were training with carbines—Elian carbines. All of these men could take carbine hits without even flinching. They were training to fight the Elian Military. They had to be. LeMaine couldn't think of any other explanation.

LeMaine couldn't stay in the same room with them a second longer. He fled from them, but none of them even noticed him leaving. None of them looked at him once the whole time he was in the gymnasium with them. They were braindead except for their ability to fight.

He raced back up to the warehouse, returned to his position above the loading area, and concentrated on getting the hell out of here. He had to do something about this—he wasn't sure what—but he needed to escape first.

He watched for his chance, but he didn't see anything. There were too many Axichis working down on the loading floor.

In the end, he waited until darkness fell. The last vehicle was still in the middle of taking on its load when the Axichis stopped work, locked up the loading area, shut down the factory equipment, switched off all the lights and equipment in the lab, and all the Axichis left the building.

The building plunged into darkness, but LeMaine didn't care. He knew now what he had to do.

He stayed where he was until long after the building fell silent. He rested his forehead on his knees and shut his eyes, but he couldn't stop seeing all those men downstairs. They complied so mindlessly with what the Axichis wanted them to do.

It all came back to the drug. The Axichis had developed this drug to lobotomize these men and make them mindless slaves. Now these men would do whatever the Axichis wanted.

These men would even attack their own kind. They would go into battle against the Elian Military, take carbine hits to their chests and bodies, and keep on going.

LeMaine shuddered and forced himself to stand up. He climbed down to the loading floor, clambered into the one vehicle parked on the floor, tucked himself in behind a bunch of crates where no one could see him, and finally fell asleep there.

He didn't care anymore about waiting until tomorrow. He would wait as long as it took. He had to get out of here alive and in one piece. Nothing was more important than getting out of here with this information. He would stop at nothing until he took this information back to Elia.

Command would know what to do about this. It was too big for him to handle on his own.

Chapter 5

L eMaine woke up when the first Axichis voices rang through the factory the next morning. He stiffened in his hiding place, but he stayed still and quiet while the workers finished loading the vehicle.

Its rear freight hold slammed shut with him inside it. The vehicle left the warehouse and trundled through the city streets. More vehicle noise surrounded him and then all of that went quiet. Was the vehicle leaving the city?

LeMaine wedged himself out of his hiding place to find out and burrowed to the vehicle wall. It had been constructed of metal, so there was no way for him to see through it as long as the vehicle was moving.

He slid his laser rifle up, but he couldn't move very well with all the cargo packed in around him. He fired a single shot into the wall and bored a hole to the outside. No one would see that.

He peered through it at rolling countryside going past. The vehicle was driving into the mountains, but he couldn't tell in which direction. If it went to another strategic center or base, he was screwed.

He had to find a way off this vehicle before the driver discovered him. He needed to get out from behind the cargo before anyone unloaded it and found him here.

He positioned his rifle to cut a wider opening through which he could escape. He angled the weapon a little farther to each side and craved a square a foot wide.

The burned-out section fell away, but before he could crawl through and drop down onto the side of the road, the vehicle came to a stop.

The driver and another Axichis got out of the compartment, exchanged a few words, and walked away. Their voices receded. LeMaine wouldn't find a better chance than now to make himself scarce.

He forced his body through the hole, grabbed his rifle and pack, and dashed off into the trees. He dove into the undergrowth and buried himself in the thicket to hide.

He held his breath and strained his ears to make sure no one came after him, but they didn't. He pushed the branches aside to check the vehicle.

He only wanted to make sure the driver and his companion didn't see where LeMaine had gone, but LeMaine changed his mind when the two Axichis started unloading the cargo.

He noticed for the first time that the crates were all the same ones that had come out of the lab. They were carrying the drug.

The driver and his companion carried the crates to a low shed at the brow of a hill just beyond where they'd parked the vehicle. That hill dropped away to reveal open sky beyond and more mountains receding into the distance. What the hell were they doing putting the drug in a shed in the middle of nowhere?

LeMaine decided to stick around and find out. Whatever the Axichis were doing, they were up to no good.

The two Axichis finished stacking the shed long before they exhausted the cargo. They locked up the shed, and a few minutes later, five more vehicles showed up also carrying the drug.

An Axichis warship came down to land and the crew unloaded the crates into the warship before it flew away. The drivers drove away in their vehicles and left the hilltop deserted.

LeMaine stayed in his hiding place while his mind raced in a million directions. So the drug had something to do with the invasion. That made sense. The Axichis were preparing to invade Elia for the second time.

The Axichis wouldn't deploy this drug on their own people. They wouldn't be experimenting with it on humans if they planned to use it on Axichis.

They were mass-producing too much of it. That could only mean one thing. They wanted to use it on the Elian population—to lobotomize them and turn them into zombie slaves, too.

He wiped all thought of scrubbing the mission from his mind. He had to stop this plot and he could only do that here.

He waited for a long time to make sure no more vehicles came along. Then he stepped out into the open, checked his remote, and found the shortest route back to the rendezvous.

He strode down the brow of the hill on his way to the rendezvous location. He had to pass the shed, and just as he was preparing to turn away, he caught sight of something that stopped him in his tracks.

The hill dropped away to a valley below the hill on which he stood. He stood right next to the shed, and down in the valley below him, hundreds upon hundreds of humans milled around doing nothing. They didn't even see each other.

Their ragged clothes and disheveled hair gave all the evidence LeMaine needed to prove that these people had been here for a long, long time. The men had all grown thick, scraggly beards and their dull, lifeless eyes stared straight in front of them.

Men and women bumped into each other, bounced off, and stumbled on in their mindless trance. They didn't talk. They didn't look at each other. None of them showed any sign of fatigue or a desire to sit down.

They lurched in stupid, disorganized waves from one side of the valley to another. They moved between each other in no particular order, all trace of thought erased from their faces.

LeMaine's instincts told him to hide, but none of those people so much as raised their eyes to look at him. They had no idea where they were or what they were doing here.

He gulped down sickening horror....and then he spun away. He couldn't look anymore, but the sight haunted him all the long way back to the rendezvous.

He didn't get there until late afternoon. By then, he'd made up his mind. He couldn't leave those people here. The Axichis had already killed them. They were lost to Elia forever, but he wouldn't leave them here to suffer like this.

He made it to the ruin to find Nunn and Monk already there. They spun around and raised their rifles when they heard him coming. "Captain!" Monk exclaimed. "We thought we'd lost you!"

Lemon, O'Hara, Heckler, Lutov, and Tavon stood around doing nothing. Kellogg glanced over his shoulder from where he knelt next to Polasek, who lay on his back by the ruin. "We lost Galo. We don't know where Peterman and Sindra are."

LeMaine completely ignored them and strode over to Nunn. "Give me your pack."

She jolted in alarm. "Captain?"

"I said give me your pack now!" he barked. "Hand it over."

She took it off and he yanked it out of her hand, dropped it on the ground, went down on his knees, and ripped it open.

The other Hellhounds stared at him as he rifled her supplies, laid out the Plaostine blocks she'd brought, and primed them.

"Damn it," he muttered. "It isn't enough, but it will have to be."

"Captain?" Lemon asked. "What's wrong?"

"We'll need to find more. We'll have to hit one of their supply centers."

"Why?" Nunn asked.

His head snapped up and he shot her a deadly look, but when their eyes met, he was the one who looked away first. "We have a problem—a big problem."

"A bigger problem than losing one man and almost losing another?" Kellogg asked. "Don't you even give a shit about Galo and Polasek?"

LeMaine got to his feet, zipped up Nunn's pack, and put it on his own back. "Come on. Let's go. We gotta move fast."

"Hey!" Kellogg roared. "I'm talking to you!"

He stood up, left Polasek where he was lying, and strode toward LeMaine in a way that meant Kellogg wasn't screwing around.

"We don't have time for this," LeMaine insisted. "Come on—all of you. Pack up and move. We gotta get back over to that hill by dark. It's important."

"Your second-in-command is lying over there half-dead and we just lost three of our guys out there," Kellogg snapped. "You better tell us what the hell is going on or none of us is going anywhere with you."

LeMaine opened his mouth to argue back and noticed everyone staring at him. It wasn't just that they were staring at him. It was *how* they were staring at him.

What could they see? He couldn't stand them seeing that. He felt it burned into his very being even now.

He paced away from them, stopped ten feet away, and stared out at the mountains, but he couldn't unsee it. He would never get rid of it—not as long as he lived.

"Captain?" Nunn asked. "Talk to us."

Her voice burned him and he glanced over his shoulder at them all, but he had to turn away again. He passed his hand across his mouth trying to hold it all together. He had to tell them. He couldn't keep it to himself.

Kellogg stepped in front of him. "What happened?"

LeMaine couldn't look at Kellogg, either, so he turned back to face the squad. He had to keep his eyes down, though, so he wouldn't see any of them. "I have to show you something."

They all exchanged glances and then they started packing up their stuff. Kellogg put his kit away and Monk carried Polasek. He was stable enough to travel, but still weak from the injuries he sustained in the explosion.

LeMaine led them back to the hill. He didn't want to go back, but the rest of the squad had to know. He couldn't go on with this mission without them knowing everything he knew.

They had to hide and wait for more vehicles to come along and load more crates onto another warship.

LeMaine didn't allow himself to think anymore about just how many doses of the drug the Axichis were moving into position to deploy into Elia the minute the Axichis got a toehold inside the system.

Maybe they didn't have enough doses before or maybe they'd only been delaying until they secured enough of the system to control the population. It didn't matter anymore why they were doing this or how they planned to do it.

The squad made it to the hill at sunset. LeMaine approached the brow of the hill and stopped staring down at the people in the distance.

The other Hellhounds lined up next to him and Monk set Polasek on his feet. Monk kept supporting him even when Polasek held up his own weight.

"What......the.....hell......?" Heckler growled.

"The Axichis are producing a drug that wipes these people's minds," LeMaine explained. "They control these people and make them cooperate. The Axichis have a factory in the city to mass-produce millions of doses of the stuff. They're training captured human prisoners to withstand carbine fire. The drug makes them super-strong so they can go into battle against Elian forces. We have to stop them."

The squad stared down into the valley in silence as the truth sank in. No one said a word for a long time.

LeMaine wanted to leave, but he couldn't yet. This wasn't over.

It took a long time with all the people down there. They lurched back and forth in their mindless, disordered streams, bumping into each other, and moving on.

O'Hara gasped as a group of men appeared from the northern end of the valley. They stumbled right past the hill where the squad could see them.

"Is that.....?" O'Hara whispered.

More people came into view. LeMaine recognized them all. They were crews from Elian ships that had disappeared at different times in the last twenty years. Some of the crewmen had aged since they went missing. Others were still young.

They passed the hill and a tall man with dusty brown hair blundered out of the crowd. Four other men stayed close to him, but they did it out of instinct, not because they knew or cared who they were with.

"NO!!" Monk bellowed. "NOO!!!"

He took a step forward to walk down the hill. LeMaine slammed his arm in front of Monk's chest to stop him.

Nunn's voice set LeMaine's hair on end. "Mack?" she murmured and her voice instantly started to rise. "Mack! MACK!!! MACK!!!"

She lunged forward screaming at the top of her lungs. LeMaine barely let go of Monk in time to grab her. "He can't hear you!"

"MACK!!" she roared. "MAACCCKKK!!"

"He isn't there, Molly!" LeMaine bellowed in her face. "He's gone! He's dead!"

"MAACCCKKK!" she shrieked and burst into sobs in his arms. She struggled and kicked at him trying to break away and run into the valley.

He had to pick her feet up off the ground and wrestle her away to stop her from going down there. She kept screaming and crying her eyes out as he dragged her away into the trees.

Chapter 6

L eMaine sat on the ground under the trees in the dark. The Hellhounds didn't dare to light a fire unless the Axichis spotted it. Faint starlight drifted through the treetops overhead. It gave the only light for the squad members to see each other.

Lutov, Tavon, and the Hellhounds sat near him, but they didn't talk. They listened to Nunn crying in the darkness not far away. Heckler sat with her and talked to her in a low, raspy voice. No one had seen Monk for hours.

O'Hara stared down at his hands. He kept opening and closing them like he couldn't feel them.

Kellogg worked on Polasek every now and then, but mostly Polasek just needed to rest and recover from his injuries. No one else moved or spoke.

Every member of the Hellhounds had recognized someone down in that valley. Some of the Axichis' victims had been members of the Military. Others had been civilians on shipping crews or just random people from different planets.

LeMaine heaved a massive sigh. His stomach hurt, but he had to tell the squad what he knew. He couldn't ask them to continue this mission without telling them.

He summoned all his strength and turned to Lutov. "I'm sorry about your brother, son. He was a strong, brave soldier. If Elia and Imoliv ever come to peace, it will be because of him. I can't give him any higher praise than that. I'm sorry I didn't say it before. That was wrong of me to dishonor him like that."

Lutov didn't answer. He stared straight in front of him with the same dead, unseeing expression as those people down in the valley. Would he ever forgive LeMaine for this?

LeMaine felt worse about ignoring Lutov's loss and Galo's sacrifice than he did about anything else. He'd never reacted like that to losing one of his people in action.

Maybe he shouldn't be in command at all anymore if he could brush off a subordinate's death so callously.

Out of nowhere, Tavon turned to LeMaine. "Who's Mack?"

LeMaine looked down at the ground. "Mack Nunn—Molly's husband. He was Heckler's best friend—the friend he lost his first selection carrying to safety. Mack got assigned to a different Special Forces squad. The whole squad disappeared during a rescue operation seven years ago. No one ever found out what happened to them. Monk's brother was on the same squad. Edward Monk is down in the valley right now. He was in that group with Mack and everyone else from their squad."

Silence fell over the group. Lemon stared off into the darkness in Nunn's direction. Nunn hadn't stopped crying for hours. It took her years to get over Mack's disappearance and now this happened.

Kellogg finished working on Polasek, leaned his back against a tree, pulled a ration bar out of his pack, and started eating it. That was it. That was the end of the conversation.

LeMaine lost track of time. It didn't seem to matter anymore. The Hellhounds might wind up sitting here all night if that's how long it took for Monk, Heckler, and Nunn to come back.

Rustling leaves broke the silence and Monk crashed through the undergrowth. He burst into the circle, cast a scowl at his squad mates, and dropped down next to O'Hara. Monk hunched his shoulders, looked at the ground, and didn't say a word.

No sound disturbed the silence. Nunn wasn't crying anymore and Heckler wasn't talking. Everyone sat without moving for another half an hour before Nunn and Heckler returned.

Heckler kept his arm around her shoulders and O'Hara moved closer to Monk to make room for them to sit down. Nunn's face twisted in agony and she fought her mouth to hold back sobs, but the starlight still glistened on tears streaming down her cheeks.

She sat down crosslegged on the ground and Hecker sat down next to her with his arm around her while her body trembled with suppressed sobs.

"So what are we going to do about this?" Kellogg finally asked.

"We're gonna blow the valley," LeMaine murmured. "And then we're going after the warehouse where they produce this stuff. We can't stop the doses that the Axichis have already shipped out to the border, but we can free these people and stop the Axichis from producing any more of it."

Nunn started crying again, but she did it quietly.

"We can't leave these people here like this," LeMaine insisted. "They've already been used enough. It would be better for them to be dead for real than to keep stumbling around like this."

Nunn buried her face in her hands and burst into sobs. Heckler furrowed his brow and scowled at LeMaine, but Heckler kept his lips clenched shut to hold back his own despair. He wasn't angry at LeMaine for this.

"Where's the warehouse?" Polasek asked.

"It's in the city somewhere," LeMaine asked. "I didn't get a fix on its location. I was more concerned about escaping it without getting caught. I was thinking you could use his array to track some of these vehicles back to their starting point."

"My array was destroyed in the explosion. Maybe it would work better if we pulled another ambush on the vehicles and used their onboard navigation system to find the warehouse."

"Oh, right," LeMaine muttered. "I didn't think of that."

"You're right that we'll need more explosives," O'Hara went on. "The valley will take all we have now. Do you know where another supply center is?"

"Those vehicles have the Axichis equivalent of scanners," Polasek replied. "I can use them to find explosives, weapons—anything we need."

LeMaine glanced over at Nunn. She had her face uncovered. Her wild, swimming eyes darted around the circle. Did she even hear their plan?

LeMaine couldn't look at her knowing he was planning to blow up the valley with her long-lost husband in it.

LeMaine had known Mack Nunn and Edward Monk. They'd been some of the finest Special Forces soldiers in the service. He would have liked to get them into the Hellhounds, but he couldn't with Elliot Monk and Molly already on the squad. They had to serve separately.

LeMaine stole a sidelong look at Monk. He sat in the same immovable position, but his expression had hardened. He narrowed his eyes at something that wasn't there. His pain was turning to murderous determination. Now LeMaine had to figure out a way to do the same thing with Nunn.

No one said anything for a long time. There didn't seem to be anything to say.

After an hour of no talk and no movement, Kellogg pushed his pack under his head, stretched out, and went to sleep. Lutov and Tavon did the same thing, and in a little while, O'Hara scooted down his tree and propped his head on it, but he didn't shut his eyes.

No one else moved. They just sat there, hour after hour, in silent vigil for those lost but not forgotten.

When the sky started to turn a lighter shade of grey, LeMaine stood up, stretched the kinks out of his knees, picked up Nunn's backpack, and walked off alone. The others pretended not to see him go.

He returned to the hill and hiked down it. The lobotomized Elians kept walking around in their stupor. They walked all night. The drug made them strong enough that they didn't need sleep.

He joined the flow of bodies and made his way through the crowd. They didn't notice him.

The vehicle crews coming and going from the hilltop didn't notice another human down there, either. He crisscrossed the valley several times laying the charges at strategic locations where they would do the most damage.

Dense rock outcroppings dotted the hillsides all along the valley. They would become extra explosive when the Plaostine went off. The rock would create flying shrapnel and debris that would take out all these people in one hellish blast.

He laid the last charges, waited for the vehicles to clear off, and hiked back up to the Hellhounds' campsite.

All the others were on their feet including Polasek. "How are you feeling, Lieutenant?" LeMaine asked.

"I'm clear for duty, so I must be feeling pretty good," Polasek replied. "It's amazing what a good night's sleep will do for you."

"We'll need you to help us capture one of those vehicles," LeMaine went on. "I hope you're up to it."

Polasek only nodded. "Whatever it takes to defeat the enemy, Sir."

"Good man." LeMaine looked around the rest of the group and stopped in front of Nunn. "Are you ready, Sergeant?"

She nodded. Her face had swollen up and her lips were still crooked, but her expression had hardened like Monk's. She glared at everyone and everything.

He handed her the backpack that now weighed half as much as before, turned away, and walked back to the hill. All the Hellhounds followed along with the two remaining Imoliv.

They took their places looking down at the never-ending stream of humanity—what was left of it. All those people.....their bodies were here, but the people they had been were long gone—long dead in a war that started decades before anyone in Elia realized it.

Nunn started sobbing again at the sight of them all. Heckler wrapped his arms around her, kissed her on the side of the head, and turned his face behind her so he wouldn't see.

Monk went over to them and put one of his beefy arms around both of them. LeMaine pulled the remote detonator out of his pocket. He'd taken it from Nunn's pack and programmed it to all the Plaostine primers he'd laid out this morning.

He handed it to Nunn and faced the valley. He had to see this. He had to be one of the witnesses.

Her sobs got louder and more excruciating. If Mack really had been down in that valley, he would have heard her. He might even have recognized her voice, but he wasn't down there. Who knew when and where he really died? It wasn't here.

She choked on her sobs and then, with one sudden, impulsive squeeze, she fired the detonator. All the Plaostine blocks exploded in an instant. Rock shards erupted across the valley in both directions flattening all the prisoners instantly.

The shockwave trembled up the hillsides to where the Hellhounds stood. More rock split off and pounded down onto the valley floor. Whole cliff sections calved off and collapsed until the landslide buried everyone down there under a mountain of rock.

Chapter 7

N unn shot a desperate glance in both directions, raked her sleeve across her face to scrape her tears off, and shook her loose hair out of her damp eyes. She hurled the spent detonator into the valley on top of the rock pile, whirled away, and started checking her laser rifle.

She coughed and choked a few times, but all that crying and grieving was all over now. She stormed off into the trees with Heckler and Monk right behind her.

LeMaine turned to the rest of the Hellhounds. "O'Hara, you get up in those rocks over there with your rifle aimed this way. As soon as the first vehicle shows up, you shoot the driver through the front driving compartment. Do you remember where it is?"

"Yep." O'Hara replied. "I'll hit him."

"Aim high so you don't hit any of the controls. We need this vehicle intact with all its instruments functioning."

"Don't worry about it," O'Hara told him. "I know where everything is and I won't hit anything."

"Tavon, you take Lutov over there with Lemon. Kellogg, Polasek, and I will take this side. As soon as O'Hara takes out the driver, the six of us, Nunn, Monk, and Heckler will storm the vehicle, take control of it, and drive it into those trees. We'll hide it while Polasek hacks the navigation system."

"Got it," Tavon replied.

The squad broke up and O'Hara scrambled onto the rocks LeMaine indicated. LeMaine, Polasek, and Kellogg retreated and crouched behind the hill with their rifles.

The two Imoliv found a patch of bushes directly across from where the vehicle had dropped LeMaine off two days ago. If this worked out, the first vehicle would be earlier than all the others.

LeMaine stole a peek toward the forest. Nunn crouched in there with her rifle to her eye. She looked as fierce and determined as Monk and Heckler. None of those three would be taking any prisoners on this mission.

The squad didn't have long to wait before LeMaine heard engine noise coming closer. It came from behind the trees, and pretty soon, a single vehicle sailed into sight.

It pulled up on the hilltop and stopped in the usual spot with its engine running. The next minute stretched into eternity. What was O'Hara waiting for?

Just then, the engines cycled up to a higher pitch and a laser erupted from the rocks, pierced the driving compartment, and LeMaine vaulted out of his hiding place.

The three flanks closed on the vehicle. LeMaine yanked open the driver's door at the same time Lutov yanked open the passenger door on the other side. Tavon, Lemon, Kellogg, and Polasek aimed their rifles into the compartment over LeMaine's and Lutov's shoulders.

The driver sat in his seat with a perfectly round laser burn through his left eye. It was a once-in-a-lifetime shot considering O'Hara hadn't even been able to see the driver through the compartment wall. The engines were still running.

LeMaine seized the driver and dragged the body out. "Get the vehicle away now!" he ordered and started hauling the body toward the brow of the hill.

He got the body to the very lip of the drop-off before he heard more engines approaching from the same direction. Polasek leapt into the driver's seat, grabbed the controls, and ripped the vehicle backward.

The squad scattered as the vehicle exploded into a full-speed sprint for the trees. Polasek buried it in the undergrowth just as another vehicle came burning around the bend.

The Imoliv ducked behind their bushes and Kellogg sprang over the brow of the hill to hide. LeMaine flung the body down on the rock pile and dropped out of sight just in time.

No one moved or made a sound as the second crew unloaded and more vehicles showed up to do the same thing. LeMaine sure hoped Polasek was making some progress on the vehicle.

Fortunately, none of the Axichis noticed anything out of the ordinary. They were too busy loading their cargo onto the warship to look over the side of the hill.

Eventually they all left and LeMaine snuck out of hiding. He and the rest of the squad went into the trees and O'Hara climbed down to join them.

They found Nunn, Heckler, and Monk standing guard while Polasek sat in the driver's seat fiddling with everything. "Any luck, Lieutenant?" LeMaine asked.

"I found the warehouse," Polasek replied. "I'm going to remove this navigation system when we leave here. We can use this as a remote array. We're too deep in Axichis space for it to work for communications, but we can use it to navigate between the warehouse and wherever we get our additional supplies."

"Where *are* we getting our additional supplies?" Lemon asked. "That's going to be a mission all its own."

LeMaine turned to O'Hara. "Congratulations, Sergeant. That shot was incredible."

O'Hara beamed at him. "I told you not to worry about it."

"He's right, O'Hara," Nunn chimed in. "You're the best there ever was."

O'Hara blushed. "Be careful. You don't want to inflate my head any more than it already is."

"I think you deserve to inflate it a little more after that shot," LeMaine replied. "I'm gonna have to come up with a way to reward you for that one."

"How about you just don't tell anybody?"

"No way!" Lemon countered. "You could get the Zukion Star for a shot like that."

"Just the squad knowing about it is enough," O'Hara replied.

LeMaine studied him for a second. O'Hara said that in a soft undertone. He really meant it. He didn't want anyone to find out just how good he really was. His squad mates' praise was reward enough.

Polasek drew LeMaine's attention back to the mission. "I got it. There's a supply depot south of town."

"Can we take the vehicle?" Nunn asked. "It won't take as long that way."

"What do you think, Polasek?" LeMaine asked.

Polasek studied the navigation system. "It sure beats walking. We need to get this done if we want to blow the warehouse."

"All right, Hellhounds," LeMaine decided. "Climb in the back."

Everyone got in and pitched the crates into the forest. Monk got behind the wheel with Polasek next to him.

They soared away across the landscape and pulled the vehicle to a stop on another hillside south of town.

LeMaine climbed down with the others and they observed the supply depot in the distance. "How do we get inside?" Lemon asked.

"It would be helpful if we could take this vehicle inside to load our stolen stuff in," Heckler pointed out.

"There are other vehicles going in and out." Polasek pointed to another route coming from the city.

The same process repeated that the squad observed at the first strategic center. Vehicles drove up to the gates, went inside, and left from the same location. Sentries searched each vehicle before it entered.

"So are we stealing another one of them?" Lutov asked.

"Do you want to take a walk, Lemon?" LeMaine asked.

"I could do that," she replied. "I won't cut the fence like I did last time, though."

"What are you going to do?" Monk asked.

"I think I might get a little payback while I'm in there. These jackasses need someone to send them a message."

"They don't know we're here," Tavon pointed out.

"Yes, they do," LeMaine replied. "They followed me after they hit our vehicles with those rockets. They know we're here. If you want to make a statement, go right ahead."

Lemon pulled off her fatigues. The Imoliv squad members watched in fascination as she pulled her disguise suit over her head and disappeared into the grass.

"Now we wait." Kellogg sat down and went through his pack. "I'll need to stock up on medical supplies while we're in there."

"They probably don't have Elian medical supplies," Sindra remarked.

"They have Elian everything else," Monk pointed out. "They've been hoarding Elian supplies and technology all this time. They played us. That's all there is to it."

"Not anymore," LeMaine growled. "They won't get away with....."

A deafening boom went off inside the supply depot, and the next minute, a mushroom cloud of fire and smoke erupted into the sky.

"Holy shit!" Monk yelled.

"I'm guessing that's the signal!" Heckler called back.

"She better not have blown up all the explosives!" Nunn added and the Hellhounds took off for the depot.

They headed for the front gate and found it deserted. All the sentries that had been guarding it ran off into the depot before the Hellhounds got there.

Lemon materialized out of thin air just as the Hellhounds approached. She grabbed the gate and hauled it back to let them in. "Follow me!"

She dashed off through the depot. The squad skidded around corners dodging Axichis soldiers, but they were too interested in finding the source and cause of the explosion. They didn't see the squad until Lemon guided everyone into another warehouse.

A line of four vehicles sat parked inside the loading doors. Racks and racks of supplies rose to the ceiling.

"Holy crapsticks!" O'Hara murmured. "These are all Elian Military supplies!"

"Go to work, Hellhounds! Kellogg—you restock and take whatever you need. Nunn, you load that vehicle with all the explosives you can. You help her, Monk. The rest of you come with me. We're getting the weapons."

LeMaine found the racks piled with Elian carbines, and right next to that, he located another several racks of Axichis laser rifles.

"Stick with laser rifles," he told the squad. "The Axichis might have made themselves invulnerable to carbine fire, too."

The squad got to work with a vengeance, backed the vehicles up to the racks, and worked themselves into a sweat loading everything up.

Lutov and Tavon stood guard by the doors to hold off any Axichis. Lemon helped with the rifles for a while and then slipped away in her disguise suit.

LeMaine concentrated on getting the supplies out of here before the Axichis figured out what was going on. He worked fast, but not fast enough.

More explosions went off—closer this time—and then laser fire burst out somewhere. That sound jolted him to high alert. He looked up to see the two Imoliv striding out of the warehouse with their rifles up.

Lemon backed toward them and all three of them moved into line firing at something outside. Lasers skittered through the open loading door.

"Mount up!" LeMaine yelled to the others. "Drop what you're doing and get out now! Take everything back to the rendezvous!"

He checked just long enough to see Nunn, Heckler, Monk, and O'Hara climb into their vehicles. Kellogg and Polasek climbed in with them.

LeMaine dashed forward to join Lemon and the others. He took his place between Lutov and Tavon. They all exchanged fire with a bunch of Axichis advancing from their left.

"Move forward!" LeMaine ordered. "Cover the vehicles!"

The four of them inched forward a little farther. They formed a semi-circle around the loading doors and Nunn's vehicle shot away loaded with explosives.

The next two vehicles zoomed past and the Axichis turned their weapons on the fleeing vehicles. "Forward!" LeMaine roared.

He charged the Axichis. They had taken a position behind a low building and tried to skirt it to shoot at the vehicles driving away.

LeMaine raced around the building and bombarded the Axichis from their rear. They had to turn back, but that exposed him directly to their laser fire.

Lasers smashed into the walls near his head and made him duck. He had to stop shooting long enough to race behind a different corner, but that instant of delay gave the second two vehicles enough time to get out of the depot.

Monk floored the fourth vehicle. Lemon and Lutov tried to pull the same maneuver to cover Monk's escape. They ran into the gap between LeMaine and the Axichis and opened fire.

Their maneuver worked. The Axichis turned their backs on Monk's vehicle to assault the two Hellhounds instead, but at that instant, some other projectile whistled from somewhere out of sight. It smashed into the back end of Monk's vehicle and it skidded wildly out of control.

He fishtailed for a second, fought it into a straight line, and then erupted in a burst of speed that carried the vehicle out of sight.

That left LeMaine and his three comrades alone at the depot with all the Axichis. Lutov and Tavon advanced from the side, but the building gave the Axichis enough cover from those two.

Lemon backed toward LeMaine and then an unholy blast of laser fire bombarded the area from LeMaine's right. He didn't see any Axichis over there until the building next to him dissolved in a cloud of dust.

The shockwave struck him and knocked him away. He had to shut his eyes and he took off running with no idea where he was going.

He broke through the haze, squinted just enough to avoid running into anything, and raced for any kind of cover. He was all alone in Axichis space.

He darted behind another warehouse. He had to find a way back to the rendezvous point, which meant he needed a vehicle, but he couldn't leave his comrades behind. Where were they?

Gunfire led him back toward the warehouse the Hellhounds had raided. The firefight came from behind him.

He skimmed walls, sprinted across intersections, and crouched behind more vehicles trying to see where the conflict was. There was no shortage of vehicles around. He could steal one of them, but that would only alert the Axichis to his location.

He got behind a building where the gunfire sounded the loudest. It sounded like it was coming from right on the other side of the building. Who was over there? Was Lemon in trouble....or Lutov?

Right then, the gunfire cut off. The depot fell silent except for Axichis voices talking to each other.

LeMaine tiptoed closer and peeked around the building. He didn't see anything except a bunch of Axichis standing around discussing something. They pointed toward the west—toward the rendezvous point. Did they catch up with the other Hellhounds already?

He surveyed the area, but he didn't see any sign of Lemon or the two Imoliv. There was nothing there but Axichis.

LeMaine didn't dare to go any closer. He skirted his building, but he still didn't see anything. He had to find his people. He couldn't leave them in danger.

He retreated, made his way back to the warehouse the Hellhounds had raided, and then covered as much of the depot as he dared before he returned to the same spot.

The same group of Axichis were still there. Lemon and the Imoliv were still not there. LeMaine frowned to himself. They didn't just vanish. They'd been in a firefight against the Axichis just a few seconds ago.

Well, Lemon might have just vanished, but she wouldn't leave the others in danger. No way. Was it possible she'd found a way to disguise all three of them? She couldn't have done that with only one suit.

LeMaine's brain started to go in some strange directions, but there was nothing more he could do here. He started looking around for a vehicle to steal. He would have to go back to the rendezvous and meet up with whoever had escaped.

Maybe Polasek could modify one of the vehicles' navigation systems to locate any human and Imoliv life signs on this planet. That shouldn't be too difficult. The Hellhounds were the only humans and Imoliv around.

He started to walk away when more Axichis voices made him look back. He froze and crouched in place when a bunch of Axichis marched Monk and O'Hara into view.

The Axichis held them at gunpoint and then, for no apparent reason LeMaine could see, one of the Axichis clubbed O'Hara across the back of the head.

O'Hara buckled and hit the ground. Monk surged forward to intervene, but more Axichis held him back.

The Axichis who hit O'Hara swiveled his rifle to his shoulder and pointed it at O'Hara's head. LeMaine had been in combat too many times not to recognize that this Axichis really was about to blow O'Hara's brains out.

LeMaine reacted instantly, raised his own rifle, and fired. His laser exploded the Axichis gunman's head in a cloud of pulp and that drew the rest of the Axichis to LeMaine's location.

Unlike carbine fire, these laser rifles gave a perfectly straight line directly to the gun that fired that laser. All the Axichis split off to hunt LeMaine down.

He sprinted away to take cover in the depot, but he didn't regret saving O'Hara, even if it only lasted a few minutes before all the Hellhounds lost their lives anyway.

LeMaine gave the Axichis the runaround for a while. He didn't have any trouble avoiding them, which should have been strange considering they had the technology to pinpoint his life signs no matter where he went.

He eventually circled the depot and came back to the same spot where the Axichis had brought in the two Hellhounds. He got there just in time to see the Axichis loading the two men into the back of a vehicle. Monk had to help O'Hara.

The Axichis kept pointing toward the west. The Axichis must be tracking the rest of the squad. Monk had been in a vehicle by himself. O'Hara had been in the next vehicle in front of Monk. That meant Nunn, Heckler, Polasek, and Kellogg were still out there....hopefully.

LeMaine made up his mind not to let these two out of his sight. The Axichis pulled another four vehicles into convoy with the one carrying Monk and O'Hara. The Axichis left the convoy unguarded just long enough for LeMaine to slip on board one of the vehicles and hide himself.

Chapter 8

The vehicle in which LeMaine hid zoomed over the landscape. He used his laser rifle in the same way and burned a hole in the side wall so he could peek out.

The Axichis drove their convoy back into the city. Were they headed back to the lab?

They must be taking Monk and O'Hara to join the other Elians that LeMaine had seen at the lab. LeMaine couldn't let himself get taken into the warehouse on board this vehicle. He needed to get off it before then. Then he could sneak into the warehouse unseen.

He couldn't see enough through this little hole, so he worked his way to the rear of the vehicle and opened one of the back doors a crack. He couldn't be certain where in the city he was, but after a while, the vehicle turned into a few different alleys. It took a back route to the warehouse. This would have to be good enough.

He jumped out and ran off into the neighborhood while the convoy kept going. Now he had to find the warehouse.

He hunted around for a while until he thought he found the alley he'd been hiding in when he first discovered the lab. He climbed the stairs into the same dusty abandoned upper story. From there, he made his way back to the mezzanine just as the Axichis drove their vehicle into the warehouse.

The Axichis pulled Monk out of the back of the vehicle. The Axichis had to drag O'Hara out and they dropped him unconscious at Monk's feet. None of the Axichis stopped Monk from kneeling down to check on O'Hara, but Monk couldn't help O'Hara. They had no medical supplies or equipment.

The Axichis exchanged a few words with Monk. He lunged forward again and again the surrounding Axichis soldiers stopped him. The Axichis marched Monk away. The Axichis had to drag O'Hara, one under each of his arms.

LeMaine had to scramble to follow them. The Axichis didn't take the two Hellhounds to the lab or to the underground gymnasium. They hauled the men down a few more flights of stairs, exited on one of the disused lower floors, and into a dark hallway. LeMaine couldn't follow them there.

He itched to talk to them and tell them he was here, but he had to wait for the Axichis to leave.

He retreated to the mezzanine to watch and think. The Axichis would bring any captured Hellhounds back here as long as the Axichis didn't kill them first.

LeMaine decided to wait for nightfall when the Axichis shut down the lab and the warehouse. Then he would find a way to contact the two Hellhounds locked up under this building. He had to find a way to free them before the Axichis dosed Monk and O'Hara with the drug.

Nothing happened for hours. He settled down in a corner and turned his thoughts to the problem of getting his people out of here. Breaking them out, stealing a vehicle, and then finding a way off this planet shouldn't be too hard.

He still had to blow this lab, and for that, he needed explosives. Did Nunn get away with her load? Did she hide it somewhere in the countryside?

One Axichis rocket would have blown her and the load to kingdom come. The whole operation of stealing those explosives might have been for nothing.

He pushed that thought out of his head. He couldn't start thinking like that. He had to keep believing that Nunn was hiding out in the mountains somewhere with a load of explosives big enough to take down this lab and everyone in it.

The day wore on and he stopped watching the activity down on the warehouse floor. He glanced up when the prisoners from the basement started filing into the lab for their daily dose of the drug. Did they need regular doses to keep them docile?

He didn't see the Axichis giving those poor unfortunates in the valley regular doses. The Axichis completely ignored them and the prisoners just kept lumbering around in their stupor, but why else would the Axichis keep so much of the drug in that shed? What else could it be for if not to dose the captive Elians?

They might have been under the drug's influence for too long. Maybe these guys in this building could still be saved....but how would LeMaine get them away? There were too many of them and they wouldn't be much help fighting the Axichis.

He went back to staring at the wall and was just getting ready to shut his eyes when a shout made him look up again. He jumped onto his knees and raised his rifle when another vehicle pulled into the warehouse.

The Axichis pulled Lemon out followed by Lutov and Tavon. Lemon wore her disguise suit, but it didn't disguise her. The black fabric covered her from the neck down with a giant rip down the front exposing her stomach and part of her thigh. The suit must have gotten too damaged to conceal her anymore.

The Axichis shoved the three of them together in a group and held them at gunpoint, too. The Axichis went through another discussion about what to do with them and someone pointed to the lab.

One of the Axichis entered the lab and came back with a technician who pointed some kind of scanner at the two Imoliv. Did the drug work on Imoliv? That would make this interesting.

The technician nodded, went back into the lab, and the Axichis soldiers started to push the three Hellhounds away. At least they would be in the same place as Monk and O'Hara.

They all turned to head off when another vehicle pulled in. No one gave it a second glance until the driver called out to the Axichis leading Lemon and the others. The whole group halted and turned back as the driver pulled out another captured Hellhound.

LeMaine froze and goosebumps broke out all over his skin when the Axichis threw Galo on the ground. He was unconscious and covered in blood, but he was definitely still alive.

Lutov took a step forward, only to be pushed back into place by the Axichis guarding him. Lemon and Tavon grabbed Lutov to hold him back. He started to relax into his former place when, for no reason, the vehicle driver kicked Galo across the head.

His head whipped aside, but he was so out of it that he didn't respond at all. Lutov exploded out of line, tore away from Lemon's grasping hands, and charged his brother.

Lutov dropped on his knees and tried to pick up Galo's lifeless body. Lutov got his hands wedged under his brother's shoulders when another Axichis guard stormed over and kicked *him* in the head.

The blow sent Lutov sprawling. He flipped onto his back trying to sit up and the guard took two steps forward, shouldered his rifle, and blew Lutov's brains out right there on the floor.

LeMaine winced and turned away clamping his eyes shut, but it was too late. Lemon roared and plunged out of line, but Tavon grabbed her in time to hold her back.

The guard who shot Lutov strode over to the two remaining Hellhounds pointing his rifle in their faces. Lemon kept snarling and baring her teeth at him, but the Tavon wrestled her under control before the Axichis marched them both away.

LeMaine pried his eyes open in time to see two more Axichis take hold of Galo's arms and drag him after the others. The Axichis left Lutov's headless body lying there on the warehouse floor in a spray of blood.

Chapter 9

L eMaine crumpled into his corner. Sickening cold gripped his insides and he covered his face. Nothing in the world could be worse than losing his people, especially like this.

He had to get them out of here before anything else happened to the rest of them. His mind raced through all the possibilities, but he still couldn't come up with anything better than waiting until nighttime.

He didn't want to wait. He wanted to do it right now, but he had to be prudent.

He was their only chance at escape. Having one person on the outside would be better than all of them being locked up in here. He had to stay free no matter what.

His opinion became more confirmed as the day wore on and the Axichis brought in the rest of the Hellhounds. Nunn, Heckler, Kellogg, and Polasek were too sensible to resist.

The Axichis lined them up on the warehouse floor. Kellogg was still wearing his backpack. The Axichis took it away from him, searched it, and threw it in a corner before they led the last four Hellhounds away.

The Axichis came back for the backpack a few hours later. Kellogg must have convinced them that he could give the other Hellhounds medical treatment if he had his kit. So that was some small comfort.

The hours dragged by. LeMaine kept only one eye on the warehouse floor. Nothing much changed down there. All the Axichis went about their business. LeMaine would have seen if the Hellhounds came to the lab to get dosed with the drug.

He almost dozed off when the noise down on the floor changed. The workers, lab techs, and other Axichis buzzed around a little faster. Their movements became frantic and excited.

Another vehicle pulled in and all the Axichis went into a tizzy when four other Axichis unloaded. They wore officers' uniforms. LeMaine had the misfortune to deal with Axichis officers on Toreon. He didn't plan to repeat the experience.

These guys strode around looking down their noses at everything while the workers and lab techs fluttered around trying to impress them. The workers showed the officers everything and then the lab techs gave the officers a tour of the lab.

The officers strolled back out onto the warehouse floor and looked around making sure not to be impressed with anything. Everyone went to great lengths to explain Lutov's body and the mess.

The officers then gave orders and armed guards hurried away. They dragged all the Hellhounds upstairs and lined them up in front of the officers.

LeMaine's heart started pounding when the Axichis brought up Sindra and Peterman, too. Had the Axichis been holding the two men here all this time?

Both of them looked like they'd been beaten, but they both stood up straight and walked on their own. They couldn't be too badly hurt, but the Axichis didn't bring up Galo or O'Hara. They must have been too injured, which meant they were still downstairs in the basement.

The group of officers stood back while one guy in particular sauntered down the line of prisoners, inspected them all at close range, and stopped when he came to Tavon and Sindra.

The officer asked the lab techs questions. They pointed their scanners at the two Imoliv. The lab techs discussed the results with the officers and then shook their heads. They must have been deciding that the Imoliv were no good for the experiment.

LeMaine stiffened when the guards pulled Sindra out of line, pushed him down on his knees, and aimed their guns at his head. LeMaine couldn't watch another one of these guys getting shot—not on LeMaine's watch.

He threw caution to the wind and raised his own rifle, but he didn't shoot the gunmen. That would only put Sindra in more danger.

LeMaine fired into the lab. The glass windows shattered and he kept dumping more and more shots into the room. His shots struck the machinery that mass-produced that drug.

The equipment exploded and all the Axichis jumped out of their skins. They turned toward the lab and then all the guards raised their rifles to aim at the mezzanine.

LeMaine rotated his rifle down onto the floor and pounded the Axichis with heavy fire. The Hellhounds scattered. Monk, Heckler, Nunn, and Kellogg attacked the guards from behind.

Nunn and Kellogg both managed to wrestle the Axichis' rifles away and turn them on the soldiers.

So many workers ran screaming from LeMaine's fire that they confused the soldiers. No one knew what to do for a second and LeMaine cut down more guards and even a few officers.

He swiveled his rifle back toward the lab and smashed up as much of the equipment as he could. He wanted to destroy the whole building, but he couldn't do that from here.

Nunn and Kellogg got the other Hellhounds behind them, guarded them with laser fire, and the whole squad backed toward the officers' vehicle. They started to load up when a deafening smash of laser fire erupted from the opposite side of the warehouse.

It came from near the lab. LeMaine couldn't see through the mezzanine floor, but there must be another group of Axichis down there.

Their lasers smashed into the vehicle's front engines and the vehicle exploded in flames just as the Hellhounds were trying to get on board. They had no choice but to run for it.

They bolted out into the alley and scattered in all directions. LeMaine kept pounding the warehouse floor with all his fire, but now he was the only Hellhound left in the building—except for Galo and O'Hara.

LeMaine backed toward the stairs. He had to get out of here before the Axichis cornered him. He dumped a few more laser shots down onto the floor and bolted for the exit.

He dashed through the building's deserted floors, into the alley, and away. He darted around several corners before he collided full-tilt with Monk. Nunn, Kellogg, Sindra, and Tavon were all with him.

Monk grabbed LeMaine and shook him. "Captain! You did it! You freed us!"

"Not yet," LeMaine panted. "We gotta get out of here."

"There are some more vehicles over there." Nunn jerked her thumb over her shoulder. "We can get out of the city. If anyone else got away, they'll return to the rendezvous point."

"That's too far away," Kellogg countered. "We should use the vehicle's navigation system to locate the others."

"We have to get off the street either way," LeMaine replied. "Show me where the vehicles are."

The group crept back into the street. The vehicles Nunn mentioned were all civilian transports parked in front of a tall high-rise. Ordinary businesspeople went in and out. The vehicles were totally unguarded.

LeMaine pulled his people back around a corner where no one would see them. "Listen to me. Take one of these vehicles back out into the countryside. Use the navigation system to find a spacecraft to take you back to Elian space. You have to....."

"We are NOT leaving you or any of our squad mates here," Nunn snapped. "Like hell we will."

"Will you listen to me?" LeMaine whispered. "I'm going back for Galo, O'Hara, and the others, but someone has to get back to Elian space. You have to get word back to Command and to the Imoliv what's going on here. You can get around the Axichis blockade and make it back to Ziea. An Axichis fighter will blend in well enough down there. You can signal the Maczhi battalion and they'll bring you in. Getting word to Command about all this is much more important. It's more important than any of our lives. You know I'm right."

He glanced back and forth between the five of them waiting for someone to argue. Of course they didn't. They all knew he was telling the truth.

"Tavon and I will go, Captain," Sindra replied. "You'll need Nunn and Monk to help you free the others. Galo and O'Hara were both badly injured. They won't be able to help you. You'll need your squad."

"You're the perfect man for this mission, Sindra," LeMaine told him. "You can use your influence with your father to spread the word about this. The Imoliv are in danger from this, too. You saw what happened in there. The Imoliv are no good for this experiment. That means the Axichis will annihilate your people if they ever conquer the Imoliv system."

Sindra lowered his eyes and nodded. "You're right, Captain. We'll go and we'll do everything we can to send someone back to help you."

LeMaine turned to Nunn. "Did you get the explosives away?"

"Sure. We stashed two vehicles, one with the explosives and one with weapons. We hid them farther down the mountain on the west side. We didn't think we should leave them at the ruin in case someone tracked us there."

"That's perfect." LeMaine turned back to Sindra. "Nunn, Monk, and I will go out there and steal a vehicle. We'll create a diversion for you and Tavon to get out of town quietly. Get back to the ruin, unload the cargo, and take one of the vehicles to somewhere you can steal a fighter craft. Do everything as quietly and inconspicuously as you can. Don't attract any attention. Just get over the border in one piece. Nothing else matters. Can you do that?"

"Of course, Captain. I just....I hate leaving anybody behind, especially when Galo is still back there in danger."

"We'll take care of Galo. I won't let anything happen to him, especially not after the way we just lost Lutov. Now please go. That will be two men at least that I don't have to worry about."

"All right, Captain. We'll do it your way, but this isn't over. We're coming back to get you."

"Thank you, son. I really hope you make it. All our hopes and prayers are riding on you."

Without thinking about it, LeMaine stepped in and hugged Sindra and then Tavon. Both men hugged Nunn, Monk, and Kellogg. Then the two Imoliv retreated farther down the alley while Nunn, Monk, and LeMaine eyed their target vehicle.

"What's the plan, Sir?" Monk murmured.

"We get the vehicle and make a big noise to draw the Axichis away from Sindra and Tavon. Then we hide somewhere to shake off the pursuit, go back to the warehouse, and free our people."

"Sure," Nunn replied. "Simple."

LeMaine eyed the vehicles in question. No one stood near them. They sat outside the building with no one paying any attention to them, but the four Hellhounds still couldn't go out there without a dozen or more Axichis seeing them.

That just might work. LeMaine said, "Let's go," and strode out into the street.

He would have liked to conceal himself, but that wouldn't distract the Axichis from Sindra and Tavon. He walked up to the vehicle and several Axichis stopped in their tracks to gape at the Elians approaching the vehicle.

Then one of the onlookers shouted. More voices broke out up and down the street as the Hellhounds boarded the vehicle. Those voices cut off when he shut the door and all the vehicle's controls switched on.

"We got thirty troops moving from three sides!" Monk barked when he saw the navigation system. "It looks like the Axichis are distracted now! Are you sure you don't want me to drive?"

"I do know how to drive, Monk!" LeMaine yelled back and grabbed the controls.

The engines blazed to life, but instead of screaming away through the streets, LeMaine slammed the throttle back and lifted the vehicle off the ground.

The thing rocketed straight up into the air, soared over buildings, and then LeMaine blasted away at lightning speed.

"Yeee-haww!!" Nunn cheered over the engine noise. "Go, Sir!"

"You call this driving?!" Monk roared. "You're fired, Captain!"

LeMaine laughed, but he stopped when he spotted Axichis fighters weaving between the buildings on an intercept course for his position. This vehicle didn't have any onboard weapons.

LeMaine shoved his laser rifle into Nunn's hands. "Take this and shoot those suckers!"

"You got it! I'll shoot 'em, all right! Get out of the way, Monk!"

"HEY!!" he bellowed as she started climbing over his lap to get near the door. "How do you plan to shoot them?! This thing has no windows!"

She prodded and kicked him into the middle of the seat. Monk nearly squashed LeMaine making room for Nunn by the passenger door.

She braced herself, gritted her teeth, wrapped the rifle strap around her body, and threw the door open. Monk hollered again, but Nunn ignored him.

The wind whipped the door closed in her face. She had to wedge the steel toe of her boot into the crack to hold it open while she leaned out into the pelting wind.

LeMaine tried to hold the vehicle steady, but it wasn't made for flying this high off the ground—to say nothing of the door interfering with the vehicle's aerodynamics. The vehicle teetered when he rounded on the fighter craft bearing down on him.

He hit the throttle making for a grouping of three and Nunn opened fire. Lasers skittered between the fighters and the grouping broke apart.

"You crazy witch!" Monk roared. "You're gonna get us all killed!"

"Bring it back around, Sir!" she hollered. "Come at them from behind and drive them toward the city!"

LeMaine did his best to follow her instructions, but this civilian craft didn't maneuver well enough. He swerved between buildings while Nunn tried to target the fighter craft.

They could maneuver just fine. They spiraled in circles around the vehicle and peppered it with laser fire. They nearly hit Nunn and blasted the door off instead.

The shot almost knocked her out of the vehicle, but Monk seized her by the belt and towed her back inside at the last second before she plummeted to her death.

She slammed down into the seat and beamed at him. "Thanks!"

He put his hand out to take the rifle from her. "Give me that. You're gonna get us all killed."

"No way!" She sprang up and leaned out the door again. "Hold onto me!"

"Stop!!" Monk bellowed, but she was already standing up and leveling her weapon at the enemy.

He snatched her belt again, and this time, he held her there so she wouldn't fall. She pumped lasers at fighter craft wheeling all around the vehicle.

LeMaine had to work hard to avoid smashing into buildings in between dodging lasers. The Axichis kept hitting the vehicle, but they didn't disable it and they didn't try to shoot Nunn. They could have hit her a dozen times, but they fired on the vehicle's outer walls instead.

LeMaine already had a pretty good idea of why the Axichis wanted to take the four Elians alive. He didn't want to let that happen, but the thought of going back to save Galo and O'Hara changed his mind.

He spun the vehicle around and angled toward the Axichis fighters. If they wanted to keep the Hellhounds alive so bad, he would use that to his advantage.

He punched the throttle gunning straight for them and Nunn unloaded right and left. She hit four of them and exploded one.

The impact struck the vehicle sideways, and in that moment, two fighters split formation. They could maneuver so much more quickly than this stupid vehicle.

They parted, swooped around the vehicle on both sides, and two matched lasers struck the vehicle's tail.

The vehicle twirled out of control. All LeMaine's efforts to stabilize it only threatened to throw Nunn out the door.

She screamed out trying to catch her balance and Monk dragged her back into the driving compartment, but nothing could get the vehicle flying again. It spun in circles losing altitude by the second.

"As soon as we hit the ground, run for it!" he yelled to the other two. "Get away from the vehicle and get yourselves good and lost! Understand?"

"No way!" Nunn yelled. "We have to stick together!"

"Don't listen to her, Sir!" Monk roared. "I'll get her away."

"No, you won't!" Nunn countered. "You don't tell me what to....."

"SHUT UP!!" he thundered in her face. "You get ready to run and don't give me any shit! Understand?"

Nunn shrank from him. LeMaine didn't say a word. He didn't dare to argue with Monk right now.

Monk pointed past Nunn's shoulder. The vehicle continued to drift between two buildings toward a different street. "The captain gave you an order. As soon as we touch down, you run."

Nunn didn't reply. She turned around to face the street, scooted closer to the door, and leaned out still holding onto the door frame. She was going to follow that order, not because LeMaine gave it, but because Monk did. If Monk gave LeMaine an order right now, he would have carried it out with no question.

Monk inched forward behind Nunn and nodded to LeMaine over his shoulder. LeMaine nodded back and took his hands off the helm. Nothing changed. The vehicle kept floating lower and lower.

Its landing gear clunked on the pavement. Nunn rocketed out of the passenger side and Monk sprang down after her. LeMaine threw open the driver's door and sprang out at a full run. Kellogg sprang out behind him and ran off in a different direction.

The fighter craft wheeled overhead and opened fire. They smashed the vehicle, but LeMaine knew now that the Axichis wanted to take the squad alive. The Axichis wouldn't kill the fugitives.

That was LeMaine's ace in the hole—that and Sindra and Tavon. They were long gone. They would make it back to the ruin by dark. With luck, they would be back in Elia by tomorrow morning.

The Maczhi battalion would see them right. If the Elian Military didn't listen, Sehiri would. LeMaine could let go of the outcome knowing the two men were out there on their own mission.

LeMaine ran through the streets, but he couldn't get away with those fighter craft pivoting and shrieking above his head. He needed somewhere to hide—somewhere they would never find him. He also no longer had his laser rifle to defend himself in case they caught up with him.

He ran for a long way before he stopped to catch his breath. The fighter craft kept patrolling the skies. They would be able to scan for his life signs. He had to find a way to block them.

He couldn't keep running forever before he dropped from exhaustion. He'd been going for days without rest.

Another fighter burned around the nearest building and hovered right in front of him. It trained its lasers on him, but now he knew that was a hollow threat. They would have to send ground troops to capture him.

He didn't know yet how he would turn that to his advantage, but he had to figure something out.

The fighter fired into the building right next to him. The explosion of rubble and metal shards set him off and he ran for it, but as soon as he dashed into the street, he spotted what looked like a railcar not far away.

It hovered above the ground the way the vehicles did, but this one had been constructed with over a dozen vehicle cars hooked together. They didn't attach to any track. They ran over a smooth surface just wide enough for the cars themselves.

The track plunged underground and vanished under some more buildings not far away. LeMaine spotted civilian Axichis seated inside those cars.

He didn't know or care where they were going. Getting underground would protect him from the fighters and he would be able to evade ground troops much better down there.

He sprinted for the track, and as soon as the cars passed, he hopped onto the track, slid down the ramp, and plunged into darkness.

Chapter 10

Leanine skidded down a long incline and slammed into something solid at the bottom. The cars' lights faded into the distance and left him blind, but at least he knew which way he had to go.

He stumbled in that direction, but he must have been going at the wrong angle. He bumped into the tunnel wall and fell over.

He groped his way to his feet and followed the wall one painstaking step at a time. This tunnel might hide him from the fighter craft, but it didn't get him any closer to the warehouse to free his people.

He ran through the possible scenarios on his way deeper underground. He could always follow the same track to the surface. He could hide down here until the pursuit broke off and then figure out what to do next.

He still needed to get as far away from the ramp as possible in case Axichis ground troops came after him from there.

He also didn't know when another string of cars might come down that ramp and run him over. He inched deeper into the darkness until, after what seemed like hours, he spotted a glimmer ahead.

It wasn't the headlamp of an oncoming train as he initially feared. He headed for it and it gave him the energy to push off the wall and walk normally, now that he could see where he was going.

It turned out to be an underground station of some kind. Civilian Axichis stood on the platform waiting for the car. LeMaine hid in the shadows, but he felt more human now. He could see light and people even if they were his enemies.

The Axichis ground troops might come from there, too, but he would just have to deal with that. *How* would he deal with it? He needed a weapon—one that wouldn't give away his position in the darkness. A laser would definitely do that.

He cast around, but the ramp on which he stood was nothing but some kind of smooth manufactured stone.

He heard engine noise coming from the same direction he'd just walked. Another train of cars approached him and it slowed down as it neared the station.

He plastered himself against the wall and found a tiny, indented alcove. He wedged himself into it as the string of cars shrieked past him in a gust of wind. The train left just enough space between the cars and the tunnel wall so he didn't get squashed.

The cars took the passengers on board, pulled away, and left the platform empty. No Axichis ground troops came down here to hunt for him, so he took a chance and climbed up onto the platform.

He didn't see anything here he could use as a weapon, either. He turned away to go back to his hiding place when he happened to look up.

Metal grilles covered the brilliant lights above the platform. The grilles had been constructed of thin metal slats positioned one on top of the other like the fins of a vent.

His heart leapt. Now he just had to find a way to take this apart so he could turn those slats into a weapon.

An inch of space separated each slat from the one next to it. He jumped, wrapped his fingers around three of the slats, and let his weight fall against them.

They creaked and bent out of shape, but they didn't break. He held on as the thin metal dug into his palms and fingers. He didn't want to hurt himself when he had no way to fix any wound, but the sharp edges gave him hope. This would be perfect if he could just get it loose.

He hung on, gritted his teeth against the pain, kicked his feet, and finally swung his weight as hard as he could trying to yank the slats free.

He almost gave up when he heard a shout down the tunnel. It came from the ramp he used to get down here and spotlights pivoted and wheeled from out in the darkness. The Axichis were coming for him.

He gave an almighty twist, and just as he was about to let go and run away, the whole grille tore out of its socket. LeMaine and the grille slammed down on the platform and the shouting got louder. The spotlights wobbled faster. The Axichis were closing in.

He snatched the whole grille, bolted into the darkness on the other side of the platform, buried himself in the darkness, and watched from the shadows.

The Axichis slowed as they approached the platform from the other side. They switched off their lights and searched the platform with their weapons shouldered.

LeMaine's heart hammered out of his chest. He had to find a way to escape from these troops. He couldn't keep running down these tunnels. He needed to be close to the ramp so he could get back out into the city streets when night came. He needed to make his stand here.

He attacked the grille with both hands, but he had to be even more careful not to cut himself. The slats were much sharper than he first realized.

His weight had wrenched one of them almost out of its socket, but he couldn't hang from it here.

The Axichis gathered on the platform, pointed at the exposed light without a grille, and then aimed their lights up the tunnel in his direction. They would be here any second now.

He put the grille on the ground, planted his foot on it, and heaved at the slat with all his might. It popped out and the sharp edge sliced his palm.

He stifled a roar of pain and slapped his hand against his pants to stop the bleeding. He didn't have time to tie up the wound before the Axichis hopped back down onto the ramp, switched on their lights, and headed for him.

He made a split-second decision and pulled out a second slat. That one cut him, too, but he honestly didn't give a shit anymore. He had a weapon—two weapons, actually. Now he had to put them to use.

He retreated farther into the darkness and patted down the walls until he found another one of those indented alcoves. Maybe the Axichis built these especially in case someone got lost in the tunnels.

He held his breath waiting for the Axichis to come near him. He took those few minutes to pull off his belt and wrap it around his palm to stem the flow of blood.

The tightness gave him a perfect grip to hold the slats. He didn't have to worry about them cutting him again.

The Axichis inched nearer angling their lights in all directions. They covered every part of the walls and ceiling. They would see him as soon as they came near enough.

He tensed for that moment and strained his ears to listen to their footsteps coming closer. His heart threatened to explode through his ribcage. He would have one chance to do this or he would be dead.

The Axichis on this end of the line drew level with LeMaine's hiding place and the light blasted LeMaine in the face. He lunged out of the alcove just as the soldier yelled out.

LeMaine hit him full force, slapped the light out of his hand, and dove for the guy's throat. The soldier had been holding his rifle in one hand and the light in the other. He didn't have time to raise his weapon before LeMaine slashed his blade across the soldier's neck and darted on.

All the other Axichis whirled around and their lights snapped to the soldier floundering on the ground with his hands clutched around his throat. None of the soldiers saw LeMaine revolve around their group, attack the guy with the second light, and slice his neck from behind.

This soldier remained standing, dropped his light and his weapon, and grabbed at his throat with both hands. All the others spun around to stare at him. Two of the remaining soldiers had spotlights. The last two didn't.

LeMaine hid behind his second victim and snatched the laser rifle that hung from the guy's shoulder. LeMaine used him as a shield, wrenched up the rifle under the guy's elbow, and fired at the two remaining lights.

Both soldiers went down and LeMaine sprinted away as fast as he could. The last two soldiers both fired at the place where the lasers had come from. They ended up hitting their friend who buckled to the floor with a thud.

All four lights lay on the ground. They reflected their beams pointed at the walls. That light gave enough illumination to show LeMaine everything he needed to see.

The last two soldiers stayed where they were pivoting their rifles in all directions trying to see where LeMaine had gone. He retreated down the tunnel into the darkness where they wouldn't be able to find him. He hid there while the last two soldiers shone their beams in his direction.

They held a hasty, whispered conversation about what they should do. They must have been under some orders to report if they found him because they slowly started to back away. They never once thought to take their dead comrades' weapons with them.

The two soldiers kept their rifles aimed down the tunnel, backed up past the platform, and then turned to hurry away to the ramp.

LeMaine stayed where he was until he knew for certain they wouldn't come back. This project worked out better than he hoped. He now had four laser rifles and two spotlights.

He returned to the bodies of the soldiers he killed, searched them, took all their weapons, and a few other supplies. The first one had a first aid kit that he used to tape up his hand and stop the bleeding. He could put his belt back on now.

Some bright spark farther up the chain of command must have had the idea to stop all traffic into the tunnels as long as the fugitive Elian was hiding down here. No more cars came...and no more ground troops or passengers came, either. The Axichis must be planning a major offensive to drive him out of the tunnels.

He gathered up his weapons and supplies, made a makeshift backpack out of one soldier's jacket, and returned to the ramp. The trip went much quicker, now that he had spotlights to show him where he was.

He made it back to the ramp at dusk. As soon as darkness fell, he would find his way to the warehouse and figure out a way to free his squad. It would have been better if he could have gotten into the building before dark, but he'd already tipped his hand on that one.

Maybe he could find some other way to make up for it. He put the spotlights away and climbed back up to the street.

Not as much foot and vehicle traffic passed at this time of day. He returned to the alleyways without any interference. The fighter craft were also gone. These Axichis weren't the sharpest tacks in the box if they let him walk around freely like this.

He hunted around and found the neighborhood with the warehouse in it, but he didn't dare to approach it from the ground.

He selected a not-so-tall building, entered through the back, and took the stairs to the roof. Most of the buildings in the city had connecting bridges between their upper floors. He didn't have any trouble getting from one roof to the next until he stopped on the roof next door to the warehouse.

He sat down in a corner to wait for dark. He didn't even know which Hellhounds were still inside apart from Galo and O'Hara. Those two were enough.

He leaned back against the wall and watched the sky go dark. He'd never worked alone this much before. It felt strange not having the Hellhounds to talk to in these moments of quiet. He wasn't used to quiet at all. They were all such loud-mouths and wise-asses.

He chuckled to himself thinking about them, but he stopped when he remembered Lutov. The young man's loss weighed heavily on LeMaine even though he knew he couldn't have done anything to save Lutov. Lemon and Tavon had tried to hold Lutov back. He would still be alive now, but he tried to help his brother.

Seeing Galo alive must have been too much for Lutov, and then to see Galo being brutalized while he was already injured.....

LeMaine shut his eyes and gulped down despair. Lutov wouldn't even get a proper military burial. The squad would never be able to take his body back to his people.

LeMaine had to get Galo out of here. LeMaine sensed Lutov calling on him from beyond the grave to save Galo. That was what Lutov would be telling LeMaine to do if Lutov had been here. Lutov would sacrifice himself to rescue Galo.

LeMaine waited until darkness fell and then crawled to the edge of the roof. He watched the last few vehicles leave the drug factory. Then the workers left, locked the loading area doors, and shut off the lights.

The Hellhounds were underground along with all the other Elian prisoners. LeMaine couldn't do anything for all the people the Axichis had already captured. He had to concentrate on rescuing the Hellhounds. That was his mission now.

Chapter 11

LeMaine waited an hour just to be sure the warehouse was totally deserted. He didn't trust for a second that he wouldn't find more armed Axichis downstairs guarding the Hellhounds.

He only hoped he wasn't too late. The Axichis might have already started dosing the Hellhounds with the drug.

He couldn't let that happen. He found another connecting bridge, crossed to the warehouse, and slipped down into the building's topmost story. It was also deserted. He descended several floors and double-checked the warehouse. Two half-loaded vehicles sat in the loading area.

The lab area had been cleaned up, but the lab hadn't been reconstructed. That was not good. The Axichis must have set up their operation somewhere else.

He found the internal stairs leading to the underground levels and returned to the floor where he'd seen the soldiers take the Hellhounds into the dark hallway.

A single door separated him from that hallway. He readied his weapon to meet whatever threat might be waiting for him on the other side of it.

He put down his homemade backpack, raised two laser rifles, one in each hand, and aimed for the door. He decided to kick in the door and unload on everyone inside, but he changed his mind and fired through the door instead.

Yells and crashes echoed from inside. LeMaine stood his ground and kept rotating his shots up and down and from side to side as he carved the door to scrap metal.

The screams died. Now he could kick the door in. It slammed open. Seven dead Axichis lay sprawled on the floor in smoking puddles of blood.

He eased into the hallway and switched on his spotlight. The beam shone on solid metal walls much sturdier than the rest of the building. Thick, reinforced metal doors with no windows lined both sides of the hall to its very end. There must be twenty doors on each side.

LeMaine stepped over the dead bodies trying to see any sign of where the Hellhounds might be, but all the doors looked the same. He would just have to open them all.

He started at the end nearest where he entered. He used his laser rifle to slice through the thick bolts locking the doors in place. He had to cut through four bolts per door.

He unlocked the first, pulled the door open, and it boomed back against its frame. He shone his light inside. A single human skeleton lay crumpled in the back corner of a tiny, windowless cell. Did the Axichis leave this person in here to die or did the person die from the drug?

LeMaine moved on and unlocked four more cells that were all empty, thank God. He made his way farther down the line one cell at a time. Two others contained skeletons—all human.

He stopped at the sixth cell on the left side of the hall and started the process all over again. How much time did he have left before sunrise?

He sliced through one bar.....then two......The process took way too long, but he had to find out where his people were.

He hauled the door open and his spotlight fell on Peterman, Polasek, Lemon, and Heckler bending over O'Hara. He looked pale, but he was conscious and sitting up. He didn't look too bad considering he'd been locked up in here for three days.

"Captain!" Polasek gasped.

"Come on!" LeMaine waved to them. "We gotta get out of here! Where are the others?"

"They're in here somewhere," Peterman replied. "The Axichis brought us all down here together."

"Never mind. Take these." LeMaine handed out his last three laser rifles and gave the two slats to Lemon and Heckler. Then he pointed to the remaining doors. "Use your rifles to cut these locks. We gotta work fast."

The four gunners spread out, one gun to a lock. LeMaine's heart skipped a beat, now that he'd found some of his people. Now he just had to find Kellogg, Nunn, Monk, and Galo. LeMaine only prayed they were together.

He cut through the locks on his door, but that cell was empty, too. He turned to the next door when Heckler called, "Found 'em!"

He darted into a cell and everyone gathered around as he helped Galo out. Kellogg emerged next carrying his backpack. "How's the patient, Sergeant?" LeMaine asked.

"He's still weak, but anything is better than staying in here."

"Right. Let's get out of here. Follow me."

LeMaine led the way back out to the stairs, up to the warehouse, and down to the loading floor. "Help me unload this cargo. We can take one of these vehicles out of town."

Heckler, Polasek, and Kellogg climbed into the back. O'Hara and Lemon got into the cab and fired up the engines.

LeMaine had to control himself not to start shaking with excitement. He was getting away with his people. They would be safe as soon as he took them out of the city.

He and the other Hellhounds tossed crates of the drug onto the warehouse floor. He didn't care anymore about making a mess.

Peterman helped Galo climb up, and as soon as the others cleared enough space, lowered Galo into a sitting position in the corner. He really did look and act weak.

Did he know about his brother? He must know by now. LeMaine couldn't imagine the other Hellhounds not telling him the truth.

The four men got halfway through tossing the cargo out when more shouts shattered LeMaine's excitement. He froze to listen just as a bunch of Axichis stalked around the vehicle aiming their rifles into the rear compartment.

LeMaine and the others froze and then slowly, slowly started to raise their arms. LeMaine looked around frantically for some way out.

His resolve hardened when the same officer strolled into view and sneered up into the cargo compartment. He read the situation in a flash.

He waved his hand and opened his mouth to say something when laser fire exploded from the other side of the warehouse. LeMaine didn't see where it came from, but it made all the Axichis duck.

Lightning quick, the vehicle rocketed off the ground, pivoted in a rapid circle, and pointed its nose toward the loading doors. More laser fire exploded from the front as Lemon unloaded on the doors.

Kellogg swerved the vehicle sideways and smashed a dozen soldiers into the wall. The office dove for cover.

"Fire!" LeMaine bellowed and snatched his rifle. He, Heckler, and Polasek opened fire from the cargo compartment and gunned down any Axichis in sight.

"Shoot!!" Lemon roared from the front.

Just as fast, the vehicle wheeled hard in the other direction and aimed its nose inward toward the building interior. That brought LeMaine and his comrades face to face with the loading door.

She had already cut it to shreds, but one rifle couldn't do enough damage.

All three men fired. LeMaine squinted into the glare as he used his laser to carve the door to pieces.

He almost toppled when Kellogg gave the vehicle another vicious jerk, whipped around in place, and punched the throttle to the wall.

The vehicle erupted forward, smashed the door out of place, and zoomed away into the night.

Kellogg skidded around corners, down streets, and hurdled buildings in a breakneck race out of town. LeMaine and the rest of the squad kept their rifles aimed through the open cargo doors for any sign of pursuit.

No one came. It couldn't be this easy....because it wasn't. The vehicle covered twenty miles of shadowy city before a punishing laser strike punched down from high orbit. None of the Hellhounds saw the vessel that fired it. It was too high up.

The shot struck the vehicle through its front engine block and the vehicle flipped upward, somersaulted in the air, and crashed down on its roof.

Crates of the drug slammed LeMaine all over his body and muffled grunts came from the men nearest him. LeMaine struggled to shake the stars out of his head.

The whine and scream of Axichis fighters coming closer woke him up in a hurry. He kicked crates away. "Come on!" he yelled to anyone who might be listening. "We gotta get out of here!"

He scrambled to his feet to find Galo and Polasek crushed under piles of crates. Heckler cradled a broken arm and blood dripped from his scalp. It got in his eyes and he blinked to clear his vision.

"Get up front," LeMaine told him. "See if Kellogg and Lemon are all right."

Heckler vanished still hugging his arm to his stomach. LeMaine got busy pulling crates off of Polasek and Galo. "Hold on, son," LeMaine panted to Galo. "We're gonna get you out of here."

Galo gave him the most hopeless look LeMaine had ever seen. Galo didn't mention Lutov, but LeMaine saw Lutov written all over Galo's face.

LeMaine couldn't look at him. LeMaine worked to clear the crates from both men and ended up tossing them onto the ground outside, too.

Heckler came back with Kellogg, who miraculously appeared unhurt. Lemon seemed fine, too.

Kellogg climbed into the back, pointed his scanner at Galo, and said, "We gotta go."

LeMaine already knew that. He left Galo to Kellogg, went over to Polasek, and dug him out of the chaos. Polasek groaned when LeMaine picked him up, but at least Polasek was still conscious.

LeMaine couldn't see anything wrong with him, so Polasek must have had internal injuries. None of that mattered now.

The Hellhounds helped the two injured men out of the back just as the fighter craft wheeled out of the city heading for the crashed vehicle.

The Hellhounds turned to the west. They were still inside the city's outer limits with dozens of miles between them and the mountains. Forget about making it back to the rendezvous point. LeMaine didn't want to go there anyway—not with the Axichis on his tail.

Where could he take the Hellhounds instead?

He rotated backward and raised his rifle to meet the oncoming fighters. Lemon appeared at his side, and a second later, Peterman and Kellogg stepped into line, too.

They backed up guarding Heckler, who supported Polasek on one shoulder while O'Hara helped Galo on the other. Heckler snarled in pain at every step. He couldn't use his injured arm to hold onto Polasek, so Polasek had to hang around Heckler's neck with both arms.

None of the three injured Hellhounds was walking too well. They limped too slowly toward the mountains in the distance. LeMaine couldn't imagine any more hopeless situation than this.

LeMaine glued his cheek to his rifle and took aim as the fighters closed in. "Get off the road!" he yelled to Heckler. "Take cover!"

LeMaine didn't turn around to see where Heckler went. LeMaine had to concentrate on the fighters.

They hurtled out of the city and turned several rotations around the group on the ground. LeMaine opened fire and the other three did the same thing.

LeMaine and Peterman concentrated their fire together on one fighter and succeeded in blowing it. It detonated in a deafening boom right on top of the group and the impact forced the other fighters to check their advance, but only for a second.

Lemon and Kellogg did the same thing. They turned their backs to LeMaine and Peterman as the fighters tried to surround the group. Kellogg and Lemon fired together at the same fighter trying to destroy it.

"Kellogg!!" LeMaine hollered over his shoulder. "Fall back with the others!! Help Heckler and the others get away!"

LeMaine expected Kellogg to argue, but he didn't. LeMaine got too occupied with shooting to see what happened next.

LeMaine's implant kicked in, but he didn't need it. He could see exactly what to shoot and where to shoot. The fighters hovered so close and so low that they gave him all the targets he needed.

He and Peterman backed up a little farther and then Lemon joined them. LeMaine didn't have a chance to ask where Kellogg was.

The fighters kept circled, firing into the ground, and trying to herd the three Hell-hounds somewhere else.

"Why don't they shoot?!" Lemon bellowed. "Why don't they try to hit us?"

"They want to take us alive!" LeMaine called back. "They've been doing this since they found out we were on the planet."

"Well, that's a good thing, then, isn't it?" Peterman asked.

LeMaine didn't have time to answer before one of the fighters fired again. The shot exploded the pavement near Lemon's feet and she sprang back.

"Break away and run for it!" LeMaine yelled. "I'll cover you!"

For once, neither of them argued, either. They kept shooting for a minute and then darted behind LeMaine. He kept backing up in the direction his squad went, but he stayed facing the fighters alone.

He pounded them with laser fire, but he couldn't destroy them on his own. He took a few steps closer and came to the mouth of an alley. He didn't see anyone behind him.

He spat a few more lasers at the fighters and took off running.

Chapter 12

LeMaine climbed out of a different underground rail ramp. It was still daylight, but the sun was going down again. He'd been hiding from the Axichis pursuit, dodging ground troops searching the tunnels, and now he was alone again.

He didn't head back to the warehouse. If he got lucky, the other Hellhounds would be waiting for him at the rendezvous. He had to find out, but he couldn't waste time walking all that way.

He went into town, did some surveillance until he found a civilian cargo transport vehicle hub, and stowed away in the back of a different vehicle heading west.

It drove out to the mountains and he jumped down once it got dark enough for him to do it unseen. Then he started hiking.

He made it to the ruin at midnight. He approached the building, only for Monk to step out of the shadows and aim a rifle in his face. "Hold it right there!" Monk boomed and then slumped. "Captain! You scared the shit out of me!"

"That makes two of us. Who's here?"

"Everyone except Peterman, O'Hara, and Lemon. Galo and Polasek are in bad shape. Kellogg has been working on them for hours. He hasn't even gotten around to fixing Heckler's arm."

LeMaine nodded and the two of them went over to the ruin. The Hellhounds were all so worried about Galo and Polasek that they barely noticed when LeMaine showed up.

Nunn squatted by Kellogg's side handing him things out of his kit. He kept snapping, "Give me that," and "Hold onto this."

Heckler sat to one side leaning against the wall with his eyes closed. He cradled his broken arm. No one had even cleaned the blood off his face. Monk was the only one free to stand guard with a rifle.

LeMaine went over to Kellogg and squatted down. "Do you want me to help you? I can relieve Nunn for a while."

"Go fix Heckler's arm if you want to do something," Kellogg snapped and went right back to work.

LeMaine did as he was ordered, took Kellogg's electrolyzer, and fitted it to Heckler's arm. He snarled through locked jaws, but he didn't open his eyes.

LeMaine centered the device over the fracture and fired it. Heckler jerked and lay still. He was out.

LeMaine returned the electrolyzer and got out the antidote. "Did anyone see what happened to the other three?"

"They were with us," Kellogg panted. "Then the fighters caught up with us. Peterman, O'Hara, and Lemon turned back to defend us. That's the last time we saw them."

LeMaine let it go at that. He gave Heckler the antidote and a dose of painkillers, left Heckler resting where he was, and waved to Monk. The two of them took their rifles back outside.

"I'll relieve you if you want to get some rest, Corporal," LeMaine told Monk.

"Hell, no, Sir," Monk boomed. "I wouldn't lie down on the job when my squad mates are in danger."

"Are the goods still down the mountainside?"

"Yep," Monk rumbled. "We unloaded it all when we got back with the Imoliv boys. They took one vehicle and Nunn and I stashed the other one in a ravine. We can take it if we need it."

"That's good," LeMaine replied. "I sure hope those boys get away all right."

"Yeah." Monk turned his eyes to the stars. "Me, too. I hope we all do." They remained silent for a while and then Monk said, "It sure is a shame about Lutov. He was a good kid."

"Yeah," LeMaine agreed. "He sure was."

"You did good getting his brother out. Lutov would have wanted that."

LeMaine nodded. Getting Galo out of that cell might not be enough if he died out here in the wilderness on some strange planet.

LeMaine and Monk patrolled the mountaintop for a long time before LeMaine went back to the ruin.

Kellogg wasn't working on Galo anymore. Now Kellogg was working on Polasek. Galo lay unconscious to one side. Kellogg had ripped off Galo's shirt, which lay in bloody rags on both sides of his bare chest.

Half-dried seals covered Galo's chest. LeMaine didn't want to think about how Kellogg learned how to operate on an Imoliv this quickly.

"How's Galo?" LeMaine asked Kellogg.

"He'll make it, but he'll be out of action for a while—a week, maybe. Sorry, but there's no way around it. It's a miracle he's alive at all."

Kellogg shot LeMaine one of those looks that told LeMaine to leave Kellogg alone and stop asking questions. Nunn also shot LeMaine a look that told him she was just as wary of pissing Kellogg off as anybody.

Just then, Heckler stood up, rotated his shoulder in a few circles, and held out his hand to LeMaine. "Give me your rifle, Captain. I'll go on watch for a while."

"If you want to go on watch, go relieve Monk," LeMaine told him. "He's been out there a lot longer than I have."

Heckler left and LeMaine nodded at Nunn. "You go get some sleep, too, Corporal. I'll take over here. You can take this as your cuddle companion."

He handed her his rifle and she gave him one of her old cheeky smirks before she walked away.

LeMaine squatted down in Nunn's place and went to work helping Kellogg. Kellogg didn't stop what he was doing for a while before he glanced up. "Thanks," he muttered.

"What for?" LeMaine asked. "Is Nunn that bad as an assistant?"

"Hey!" she yelled from across the room. "I heard that!"

Kellogg cracked a grin and wiped his blood-splattered, sweaty forehead across his shoulder. "I mean the part where you told me to fall back with the others. You saved these two—again."

"I got them hurt, you mean," LeMaine muttered. "You can save your thanks for when we all get home."

Kellogg glanced once toward Galo. "He should go home now. Seriously. I wouldn't say it if it wasn't critical."

"I know you wouldn't, but it's too dangerous now. He wouldn't be able to get onto whatever airfield might have a fighter to take him. Whoever took the fighter would have to come back here to pick him up and that would draw too much attention to this place and us. He'll just have to wait."

Kellogg nodded. "I know."

LeMaine didn't say anything. He handed Kellogg clamps, the scalpel, and everything else he needed.

Kellogg worked fast and sure. He did everything automatically in a whirlwind of efficiency to get his patients patched up as quickly as possible.

They worked for another hour before Kellogg said, "You can stand down. I don't need you anymore."

"Are you sure?" LeMaine asked.

Kellogg straightened up and stretched his back and shoulders. Polasek's chest and stomach still lay open to the night breeze. "He's stable now. I just need to close him up."

"All right. Tell me if you need anything."

LeMaine checked on Heckler and the two men stood watch until daylight. By the time LeMaine returned to the ruin, Kellogg had finished with Polasek, curled up, and fallen asleep on the cold stone floor. Kellogg didn't even take the time to wipe the blood off his hands.

Chapter 13

T he second day dawned over the ruin. Heckler, LeMaine, Nunn, and Monk took
turns standing guard, but the Hellhounds had the place to themselves.

Heckler scowled at the sky on that second morning. "It's too quiet," he growled.
"Fighters should have come for us by now."

"I agree," LeMaine replied. "The Axichis must be waiting for us to come to them."

"How do you mean?" Monk asked.

"They're holding three of our own," LeMaine replied. "The Axichis know by now that
we'll go back for our comrades. The Axichis don't need to come after us. They just have
to sit there and use our people as bait."

"What are you going to do?" Nunn asked.

"I'm going in after them, of course. I wouldn't leave them in there."

"If you go in, the Axichis will capture you, too," Heckler pointed out.

"They haven't captured me yet."

"They're bound to sooner or later," Heckler rumbled. "You can't keep tempting fate
like this."

"Heckler's right," Nunn replied. "If they know enough about us to know we'll come
for our friends, they must know enough to capture us."

"I'd rather get captured myself than leave a man behind," LeMaine replied. "The
Axichis have had their way with Elian prisoners for too long already. If we don't go in, the
Axichis will put those three down in the basement with the rest. I can't accept that—not
without doing something to stop it."

"If you get caught, they'll put *you* down in the basement," Heckler countered. "Then
what?"

"Then all you Hellhounds get yourself a ship and get the hell out of Dodge," LeMaine
replied. "Beat it back to Elia and don't look back because I'll already be dead."

Nunn looked away, but LeMaine was all done tiptoeing around the subject. He picked up his rifle, checked it, and went through the other supplies he'd taken from the soldiers in the tunnels.

"If I'm not back in two days, evacuate your wounded and retreat to Elia," LeMaine told them. "Do the same thing I told Sindra and Tavon to do. Keep a low profile, steal a ship, skirt around to Ziea, and go over to the Maczhi battalion. They'll make sure you get home."

"You aren't going back alone," Monk boomed. "Don't you dare insult us like that."

"Look," LeMaine countered. "I know we have a code of honor and everything, but...."

"We're all going," Heckler added. "You aren't leaving any of us behind."

"Will you shut the hell up for a second and listen to sense?" LeMaine snapped. "Galo and Polasek are both too injured to move, much less walk onto an airfield to steal a ship. Kellogg has to stay with them, so who do you think is going to steal the ship? Who do you think is going to be able to defend them while they get on board and who do you think is going to fly the ship back to Elian space? You three are the only ones left. It has to be you."

"And you think you're going to free Peterman, Lemon, and O'Hara by yourself?" Nunn countered. "It would be a suicide mission with all four of us. You might have done a few nice smash-and-grabs before, but now the whole Axichis force knows about us. It isn't even safe for us to stay at this ruin."

"You're right," LeMaine replied. "You should move as soon as I leave."

"Forget it, Sir," Monk countered. "No way are you going in there alone."

"Why—so we can all get captured? The more of you stay out here, the better your chances of success."

"And the more of us go in there, the better our chances of success," Heckler growled back. "You gotta admit, Captain. We're all way past the chain of command here. This is end-of-the-world-type shit. I'm not saying anything against the chain of command, but there comes a day when we all wind up floating down the same creek with the same barbed wire paddle if you catch my drift."

"Yeah, I catch your drift, Corporal. I appreciate that you want to help me, but someone has to stay here and guard the wounded. Someone has to stay out here to execute the contingency plan in case I get killed or captured. Now which of you wants to do that? It should be at least two of you if not all three."

The three of them exchanged glances. The truth was starting to sink in.

Monk finally heaved a giant sigh. "Fine. I'll stay."

"I'll stay, too," Nunn replied. "Heckler can go with you."

"All right," LeMaine murmured. "I can live with that. Can you all?"

They all nodded.

LeMaine would have liked to hug them all, but now wasn't the time. He went back inside the ruin where Kellogg was doing another scan of both patients. They were both conscious and alert.

"How are things in here?" LeMaine asked.

"About the same," Kellogg replied. "They just need to rest up and heal."

"Heckler and I are going into town to see about getting the last of our people out," LeMaine announced. "As soon as we leave, Nunn and Monk need to move you three to a different location—somewhere the Axichis won't come looking for you."

Kellogg glared at him and compressed his lips not to tell LeMaine that this contradicted Kellogg's order to let the patients rest.

LeMaine plowed right on ahead. Heckler was right. It was too late in the picture to back down now. "If I'm not back in two days, Nunn and Monk will steal a ship to evacuate you to Elia. Don't argue with me, Sergeant. Just take your patients and evacuate. That's an order."

LeMaine made sure Kellogg didn't argue back and then LeMaine walked out to go find Heckler. LeMaine wanted to get on the road. He wanted to get into town and get this mission started. If it turned out to be as much of a catastrophe as everyone predicted, that was all the more reason to get it over with quickly.

He stopped off long enough to tell Nunn and Monk to use the second stolen vehicle to transport the patients. That would save them from having to walk anywhere. Then LeMaine and Heckler took a rifle each, left Nunn and Monk to guard everyone else, and set off hiking down the mountain.

They didn't talk for hours until they returned to the flat country. LeMaine stuffed all his remaining supplies in his pocket and ripped up the soldier's jacket to make some kind of scarves that he and Heckler could use to wrap over their faces. Two human men walking around on an Axichis planet were way too obvious.

LeMaine led the way back to the transport hub and hopped a vehicle heading back into the city. LeMaine showed Heckler how to get onto a roof down the block from the warehouse.

"How did you learn to do all this?" Heckler asked. "How did you learn your way around so well?"

LeMaine snorted. "I've been on the run from the Axichis in this city too many times. I've had to run and hide and find my way into this building too often. Don't get too impressed. There's no magic to it. It was all pure dumb luck and trying to stay alive."

The two men sat down on the roof of a building three doors down from the warehouse and LeMaine leaned against the wall to get comfortable while he waited.

"It seems strange—the squad being separated all over the place like this," Heckler remarked.

"Why is it strange?" LeMaine asked. "We've done it before."

"I know. It just feels different this time."

"I'll tell you what's strange to me," LeMaine returned. "I never thought the war would take this turn. I never thought it would come to this."

"Yeah, well, I never thought I'd ever set foot in Axichis space, did I?" Heckler growled back. "This one's going in the old memoirs, ya know?"

LeMaine chuckled. "Yeah. I'm sure Peterman will have to write a whole volume on this one alone."

They both fell silent. Neither Heckler's memoir nor Peterman's great encyclopedia would ever get written if the Hellhounds didn't make it out of here alive.

"I want to thank you," Heckler muttered under his breath.

"What for? I'm just doing my job here."

"I'm talking about Mack. I want to thank you for taking me and Molly to see him. You didn't have to do that. You could have blown the valley and told us about it later....or you could have never told us at all. You could have kept it quiet. You could have told us about the drug and the experiments and the human subjects without ever telling us that Mack and Ed and their squad were down in that valley."

"I wouldn't do that," LeMaine exclaimed. "I would never keep something like that from you."

"Maybe you would," Heckler went on. "Maybe you would decide we were better off not knowing. Maybe you would decide that Molly and I had already been through enough thinking Mack was dead somewhere. You might decide that the mission was better without us knowing. You could have hidden it from us.....and you might have been right."

"Why are you thanking me, then? Don't think I don't know how much it hurt you both to find out the truth—all three of you."

"I know. That's why I'm thanking you. I'm thanking you for never bullshitting us. You've never bullshitted me once the whole time I've been under your command. You would never bullshit me or any of us about anything, not even something as important as this. You wouldn't bullshit us even for the sake of the mission. I admire that about you .....and I want to thank you for letting me and Molly and Monk blow that valley instead of doing it for us. That was a real honorable move right there.....so thank you....from all of us. I know Molly isn't good at stuff like this and I guess I'm not, either. So I guess I just want to say it from all of us."

LeMaine couldn't speak. He should have said, "You're welcome," or something to the effect that they all deserved the best he could possibly do for them.

In the end, all he felt was gratitude even to be in the presence of all of these Hellhounds. They were the most outstanding people he'd ever known in his life.

Hearing Heckler say that gave LeMaine an excruciating pang of gratitude that he was even alive to hear those words. He must have done something right even if he questioned himself some of the time—or most of the time.

He hadn't known what to do when he first discovered the valley. He'd been too confused and anguished even to think straight.

He didn't leave the actual detonation to Monk, Nunn, and Heckler out of any sense of honor or anything else. He did it because he couldn't have done it himself. He wouldn't have been able to convince himself that it was the right thing to do.

He couldn't make that decision because it wasn't his to make. He didn't have any relatives or loved ones down in that valley. He wouldn't have been able to decide at all if he did have relatives or loved ones down there.

He'd only ever tried to do his best for his Hellhounds. He'd only ever tried to do his best since his first day of basic training. He'd messed up plenty along the way. He'd made the wrong decisions and lost people even when he did make the right decision.

He owed his subordinates his best. He didn't see anything honorable or exceptional about that.

He didn't tell Heckler that, though. Contradicting anything Heckler said would have been the worst thing LeMaine could do.

LeMaine had no right to tell Heckler to think or feel anything on the subject of Mack or Molly or anything related to Mack's death and disappearance. Whatever they thought and felt about it must be right. It was their tragedy to think and feel about, not LeMaine's.

If they thought LeMaine handled it the right way, they must be right about that, too. He would never tell them otherwise. He could just rest in the relief that they thought so. That was enough for him.

He and Heckler sat in silence for a long time listening to the sounds of the city around them. Vehicles came and went on the street below their rooftop.

LeMaine planned to wait until night and then break into the warehouse again, but after another hour, a voice broke the stillness. "Captain LeMaine!!" a male voice called. "Captain Owen LeMaine!! I know you're there and I know you can hear me!!"

LeMaine shot to his feet, every nerve on high alert. He and Heckler snuck to the edge of the building and looked down. The voice kept calling out to LeMaine. It was coming from over by the warehouse.

LeMaine crossed to the next building and then to the next where he approached the parapet of the building right next door to the warehouse. The voice kept calling from directly below.

"Captain LeMaine!! Captain Owen LeMaine!! I know you can hear me!! I can wait all day for you to show yourself!"

LeMaine raised his rifle to his eye and swiveled it over the parapet. Heckler did the same thing.

LeMaine froze when he saw a whole squad of armed Axichis in the alley outside the warehouse loading door. The door had been blasted off its hinges and most of the exterior windows had been blown out. The whole building looked dark and deserted, now that the lab and all the manufacturing equipment had been destroyed.

Peterman, Lemon, and O'Hara knelt on the pavement with armed Axichis aiming their rifles at the three Hellhounds' heads.

The same officer strode up and down calling for LeMaine. He was in the act of walking away when LeMaine looked over.

"I'm right here!" LeMaine yelled back. "You can shut the hell up now!"

The officer spun around and sneered up at LeMaine and Heckler with the same look of superior disdain. "Ah, Captain! Your faithful crewmen have told me all about you and your squad members hiding in the mountains. You've given us enough trouble. We've all had enough of it."

"And you killed one of my men for no reason!" LeMaine fired back. "You would have killed all the Imoliv for no reason if I hadn't intervened."

"They were no use to us," the officer breezed. "You can understand we didn't want them hanging around."

"What the hell do you want?" LeMaine demanded. "If it's me you want, turn my people loose and I'll hand myself over to you."

The officer raised his face to meet LeMaine's gaze directly. All trace of a smile vanished from the officer's face and his features went hard as iron. "You will hand yourselves over to me—both of you—or I will kill these people of yours one at a time....and then I will kill all the rest of your people one after another until only you are left."

LeMaine glared at the man through the rifle sight. Every fiber of LeMaine's being told him to fight back, to come up with some way to avoid giving this fiend what he wanted.

There was no way out, though. LeMaine couldn't risk even one of his subordinates, much less all of them.

He lowered his rifle, dropped it on the roof at his feet, and bumped Heckler's shoulder. "Put your rifle down."

Heckler did the same thing, but he didn't stop glaring at the officer in fuming rage. LeMaine knew how Heckler felt, but there had to be a better way.

Getting taken captive by the Axichis would mean they would house him and Heckler with Peterman, Lemon, and O'Hara. With luck, being together would give them a better chance of escaping.

Or not. Nunn and Monk were still at large on this planet, but LeMaine didn't want them coming for him, either.

Standing here and watching three Hellhounds get shot was out of the question. He and Heckler made their way down to the street and around a few corners to the alley. For once, LeMaine didn't have to worry about the civilians seeing him.

The troopers grabbed him and Heckler the instant they entered the alley. The soldiers yanked LeMaine over to the officer and pushed Heckler down on his knees with the others, but they left LeMaine to face the officer standing up.

The officer resumed his disgusting sneer of contempt and triumph. "Well, Captain! That wasn't so hard, was it?"

LeMaine glared at him. No words were bad enough for this wretch. This was the man responsible for this whole hideous experiment. LeMaine knew it to the marrow of his bones just by looking into the man's face.

"Well!" the guy repeated and clapped his hands in satisfaction. "I'm Commander Aga. It's such a pleasure to make your acquaintance at last. We've all heard so much about you after you were the one who killed Commander Naelxad. You really have given us no end of trouble, Captain. We'll all be grateful to get rid of you. I can tell you!"

LeMaine didn't move. He didn't come here to be congratulated on giving the Axichis a hard time. Now that he found out just how hard a time he'd been giving them, he considered it one of the greatest compliments of his career. He would give them a whole lot more trouble before this was all over—if he survived that long.

Aga waited for him to say something, but LeMaine steadfastly kept his mouth shut. This worm didn't deserve the dignity of a response.

Aga only smirked again, rubbed his hands, and then beamed at his troops. "Well! Now that you're here, we can get started. We'll take you all back to the lab and get you started on your first doses. You can go first, Captain, since you're such a fine specimen of Elian fortitude." He laughed at his own joke. "Then we can get started on your subordinates. I'm sure they'll respond just as well as you will. Elian soldiers always respond the best."

He turned and walked away. The troops grabbed LeMaine and pushed him toward the mouth of the alley followed by Heckler, Lemon, Peterman, and O'Hara. A vehicle pulled up in the street outside and the troopers pushed all five Hellhounds into the back.

Half a dozen armed soldiers climbed in to guard the prisoners and fighter craft surrounded the vehicle as it sped away through the streets.

Chapter 14

The vehicle carrying the captured Hellhounds departed from the city around the middle of the day and whizzed over the countryside for hours. It drove for so long that LeMaine and the other Hellhounds fell asleep in the back.

The vehicle stopped once to change the guards. The current guards held the prisoners at gunpoint while someone opened the doors from the outside. It was nighttime now.

Another group of soldiers got in and held the prisoners at gunpoint while the first set dismounted. Then the first set locked everyone inside and the vehicle continued its journey.

LeMaine fell back to sleep, and when the vehicle stopped a second time, it was broad daylight outside again. The vehicle had been traveling all night.

The guards unloaded the prisoners at a prison camp in the middle of nowhere. Wide planes stretched to a different mountain range in the distance. The mountains LeMaine had gotten used to in the city were nowhere in sight.

The guards marched LeMaine, Peterman, Lemon, Heckler, and O'Hara through a tall wire fence into a camp packed with human prisoners—all of them armed.

LeMaine recognized their dull gaze and shuffling step right away. They had all been lobotomized by the drug, but other than that, they appeared healthy and robust, unlike those ragged, filthy people in the valley.

The Axichis led LeMaine and his companions to a fortified cage built into a thick stone wall on one side of the camp. The whole setup reminded him unnervingly of the base on Toreon.

The Axichis locked the prisoners in and walked away. LeMaine didn't see any other Axichis around. There was no one here but these braindead prisoners.

None of the prisoners made eye contact with LeMaine. None of them even seemed to recognize him as the same species as themselves.

He found out why pretty soon. He and the other Hellhounds collapsed on the floor. Heckler and Lemon both went straight back to sleep. O'Hara squinted out at the prisoners and Peterman came over to LeMaine. "How do you want to do this?"

"Just keep it cool for a while," LeMaine replied. "Let's just see what happens first."

"We already know what's going to happen. That Commander Aga said he's gonna dose you with the drug and then all the rest of us. We can't let that happen."

"I know," LeMaine replied. "We'll get out of here. We just need to observe and figure out a way to do it." He went over to the bars and peered around at the fence. "I don't see any guards up......"

He broke off as five of the prisoners spun around, shouldered their rifles, and aimed at LeMaine and Peterman. The prisoners reacted impossibly fast. LeMaine never would have suspected they could be so alert and trigger-happy.

LeMaine jolted away and threw up his hands in surrender. He had automatically clasped the bars with both hands when he leaned forward to peer out.

The dull-eyed prisoners stood there holding LeMaine and Peterman at gunpoint until both men backed away. Even then, the prisoners took a while before they relaxed their stance and eventually walked off.

Their expressions remained slack and their eyes lifeless through the whole episode. Those five men never once registered even the tiniest spark of intelligence or understanding of what they were doing.

LeMaine didn't relax for a long time after that. He stared after the five men and then at the other prisoners. The whole crowd of them shuffled mindlessly through the camp exactly the way the people in the valley did.

They must have been posted to guard the Hellhounds. Just to test it out, he tried again, approached the bars, and grabbed them with both hands.

The same thing happened. A different five men leveled their rifles at him until he backed off. They didn't register what they were doing, either. They'd been reduced to the status of robots.

"Do you think they're Special Forces?" Peterman murmured.

"Or regular Military. Look at them. They're all strong, fit, and well-maintained. The Axichis are keeping them in a state of battle readiness."

"What do you want to do?" Peterman asked.

"Don't go near the bars for a start."

Peterman chuckled low. "Thanks, man. I appreciate you looking out for me."

"Let's see if they ever slacken their vigilance."

He sat down next to O'Hara and Peterman sat next to LeMaine on the other side. "I don't think they will. Do you remember how it was at the valley? Those people didn't need to sleep."

LeMaine didn't answer. He remembered very well how it was at the valley. If these men didn't sleep, then the Hellhounds would have a hard time getting out of here.

The Hellhounds stayed where they were all night. He, Peterman, and O'Hara split up the watch, but the prisoners never slept. They just kept meandering around out there.

They didn't even seem to be aware that the Hellhounds were in this cage unless one of them did something that might resemble an escape attempt.

The sun rose the next day. It blistered down on the exposed camp, but the prisoners didn't seem to notice that, either. They didn't sweat or breathe heavily in the heat. Nothing touched them.

"We have to do something," Heckler insisted. "We don't know when Aga will come for you to give you the drug."

"I know that, Corporal," LeMaine replied. "If anyone has any ideas, I'm wide open."

"The back wall is the only vulnerability," Lemon pointed out. "We'll have to tunnel our way out."

"How will we do that—with our fingers?" O'Hara asked. "None of us has a tool."

"Maybe we can find some other vulnerability if we just....." Heckler went over to the wall and rested his hands on it. He moved his eyes close to the stone to study them.

Impossibly fast, a dozen armed men standing beyond the bars snapped around, shouldered their rifles, and aimed them through the bars at the Hellhounds.

LeMaine yanked Heckler away from the wall and everyone raised their hands to show the prisoners that the Hellhounds weren't trying anything.

The prisoners stared into the cell as lifelessly as ever. They didn't even seem to be looking at the Hellhounds at all. After a few long, tense moments, the prisoners lowered their weapons and ambled off as though none of it ever happened.

Heckler's shoulders slumped. "This is bad! This is really bad!"

"What about getting some weapons away from them?" O'Hara suggested. "They're all armed with laser rifles. We could use the lasers to cut these bars and then....."

"And then?" Peterman finished. "There must be more than five hundred prisoners out there. We would never get out of this cage before they cut us down."

"Well, what do you suggest?" O'Hara fired back.

Peterman glanced over at LeMaine, but LeMaine barely heard their conversation. The Axichis had stitched this one up nicely. There was no way out of here.

"Captain?" O'Hara asked. "What are we gonna do?"

LeMaine still didn't answer. He went back to his place and sat down. That seemed to be the only position in which any of the Hellhounds could touch the cage's outer walls without triggering the prisoners' threatening response.

The rest of the day passed. LeMaine and the Hellhounds kept a constant watch on the prisoners, the camp—everything. None of them saw any opening they might exploit to get out of here.

Night fell, and this time, LeMaine slept through the whole thing. What was the point of losing sleep over something he couldn't control?

He woke up on the second morning resigned to his fate. If Sindra and Tavon didn't make it back to Elia, then Nunn, Monk, and Kellogg would. They would raise the alarm.

LeMaine's trip to the Axichis system hadn't been for nothing. He'd found out about this plot. Even one of the Hellhounds making it back alive would raise the alarm.

The Elian Military Command would know how to face the Axichis from now on. The whole Elian system would realize what was at stake in terms of defeating the Axichis for good.

The other Hellhounds didn't share his opinion, though. Heckler and Lemon became increasingly agitated. By the third day, they took to wearing out the floor with endless pacing, discussing different strategies, and discarding them.

LeMaine listened with only half an ear. He could pick out the errors in their plans right away. None of the Hellhounds was going to get out of here, least of all him.

"Why don't they come for you?" Peterman asked on the third afternoon. "Aga said they would start right away."

LeMaine shrugged. "Maybe they want to mess with our heads."

Peterman turned and stared at LeMaine's profile. "Why are you giving up so easily?"

"Easily? You call this easily?" LeMaine snorted. "Maybe I shouldn't have been trying so hard."

"You know what I mean. You've never given up like this before."

"The only way to get out of here is to wait for them to unlock those bars, and even then, I don't see anyone getting past those prisoners. We're stuck in here. Admit it, Stuart."

Peterman shrugged and looked away. "There has to be a way."

"If you think of anything, I'd love to hear it."

"How can you accept your own death like this?" Peterman murmured. "That's what this is, you know. You told Molly that Mack was dead. That's what's going to happen to you."

"Thanks for reminding me."

"Did something happen to you?" Peterman asked. "Did something make you give up hope? You've never done this before."

"Yeah. Something happened. What happened was I saw that you and Lemon and O'Hara were about to get shot if I didn't give myself up. Aga could have killed me then and there....and maybe he did. Maybe my life is a small price to pay for all of yours."

"How can it be when we're looking at the same fate? If you give up, the same thing will happen to us. We need you to lead us out of here."

"I can't. I don't know how. There are some things not even I can do, Stuart. I'm only one man. I'm human. I'm not some superhero."

Peterman met his eyes once and looked away. "You're right. I'm sorry. I shouldn't have implied that."

"I wish there was something I could do. I really do. Maybe when they take me out of here, you'll see an opening. They'll have to dose me more than once. Maybe that will give the rest of you a way out. Just keep your eyes open for anything.....anything at all."

"All right," Peterman murmured. "I will."

LeMaine turned to face him. "Promise me something, Stuart. I need you to promise me something."

"What is it?"

"Kill me if I turn into one of them." LeMaine nodded through the bars. "Do for me what we did for those people in the valley. Don't leave me like that."

Peterman's face drained of all color. "Don't talk like that."

"You know it would come to that," LeMaine breathed. "You know you would want me to do the same for you. All the Hellhounds would."

Peterman gulped. He wouldn't look at LeMaine at all.

LeMaine wanted to ask again—to demand that Peterman give his promise, but something in the distraught pinch in Peterman's cheek made LeMaine hold his tongue.

LeMaine liked to think he would put down any of the Hellhounds who turned into those lifeless corpses out there. He liked to think he would do the same for them that he did for Mack Nunn, Edward Monk, and all the other people in that valley.

When he really thought about it, though, he knew he wouldn't be able to do it. He would never be able to pull the trigger on any of the Hellhounds—not ever—not even to spare them from a fate as bad as that.

He didn't even do it for the people in the valley. In the end, he left that to Nunn, Heckler, and Monk.

Hours wore on. Another night might have passed. LeMaine almost wished Aga would send for him and just get it over with.

An explosion went off somewhere and all the other Hellhounds jumped. "What was that?" Lemon murmured.

"Maybe Sindra and Tavon are coming back for us," Heckler suggested. "Maybe Nunn and Monk decided to mount a rescue operation to get us out of here."

"I hope not," LeMaine replied. "I hope they're thousands of parsecs away in Elia right now. I hope they don't even know where we are."

Dead silence answered him, but LeMaine definitely sensed a shift in the Hellhounds' mood. Heckler glared at him and O'Hara turned away—not in despair, but in disgust. They were all disgusted with LeMaine for giving up.

He couldn't even remember how long he'd been in this cage when half a dozen prisoners outside turned around and aimed their weapons at the Hellhounds for no reason. None of the Hellhounds had moved or done anything to try to escape.

The prisoners stayed where they were guarding the Hellhounds until five Axichis showed up wearing white lab coats instead of military uniforms.

LeMaine tried not to get too annoyed when he noticed that even the Axichis' lab coats were Elian make. The Axichis really did take Elia for a ride on this whole free-trade relationship. Maybe the Imoliv had the right idea with their xenophobic policies.

A shortish female Axichis unlocked the bars. "Come with us, Captain. It's time."

LeMaine stood up and faced the open cage door. The same handful of prisoners held the Hellhounds at gunpoint and more prisoners faced the cage beyond. They kept their guns down, but LeMaine couldn't deny the palpable threat of them even facing the cage.

LeMaine couldn't figure out how the Axichis were controlling these people. Maybe that was the secret—to take control of the prisoners and turn them against the Axichis instead.

He stepped forward and Lemon lunged for him. She shot out her hand to touch him. "Captain—!"

Without warning, one of the prisoners fired into the ceiling. The laser cracked off a bunch of stone shards that pelted Lemon in the face. A few larger chunks hit her in the head and knocked her to the ground.

Heckler sprang over to help her, and just as fast, two more prisoners lunged into the cell, grabbed LeMaine, yanked him out, and slammed the bars shut with all the Hellhounds still inside.

The six prisoners pivoted into line blocking LeMaine from his friends. He turned back to say goodbye to them, but before he could even open his mouth, more prisoners surrounded him, laid hold of his arms, and pulled him into the crowd.

Chapter 15

The mindless human prisoners propelled LeMaine from hand to hand getting farther and farther away from the cage where the Hellhounds remained locked up. He tried to glance back, but they were already out of sight.

The technicians in their white coats drew abreast of LeMaine and the same female said, "This way, Captain."

She said it in the most casual tone imaginable like they were out on some social excursion together. Why was she being so polite to him? Why not just cut the bullshit and acknowledge that he was about to be subjected to this drug against his will?

He cast a critical eye over the camp as he passed through it. He didn't see any way the Axichis could be controlling these prisoners. He didn't see any transmission dish where the Axichis could be programming the prisoners to do the Axichis' bidding.

Did the Axichis implant some nano-electrode in the prisoners' brains? LeMaine was about to find out.

The technicians steered him across the camp to a line of low, ugly, one-story buildings. They couldn't have looked more like labs if they'd been cut out of white paper.

They were the only buildings in the whole camp and LeMaine didn't see the prisoners even acknowledging the buildings' existence. The prisoners walked right past them without seeing them.

The technician guided LeMaine into the first one. The building consisted of one plain white room and it was empty.

LeMaine stopped in the middle of the room and looked around. "What am I doing here?"

"You're here to get your first dose of the drug," the female technician replied.

LeMaine waited, but nothing happened. He glanced down at her. "Well? Aren't you going to give it to me?"

"I just did. This room has been fitted with a special ventilation system. The drug is aerosolized into the air. You inhale it the minute you walk in. It's all over. You're done."

"What about you?" he asked. "You're breathing the same air."

She smiled at him like they were the best of friends. "The drug is calibrated to only work on humans. It doesn't work on Axichis. I can breathe it all day long. It doesn't affect me."

He didn't know what to say or what he should do. How long did he have to stay in here?

"You can go." She waved toward the door. "You can go back to the holding area with your friends."

He glanced behind him. He didn't comprehend what she meant. There were no guards around to make him go anywhere.

What if he *didn't* go back to the holding area with his friends? What if he left this building and ran for it....or found some way to turn the prisoners against their Axichis masters?

He frowned at the technician, but she only smiled back at him. She escorted him to the door, opened the door, and held it open for him to walk out alone.

He stepped out into the blazing sunshine and immediately saw his mistake. He wouldn't be able to run off or do anything else—not with all these armed prisoners standing in the way.

He took a few steps and the prisoners surrounded him. They prodded him and steered him into the crowd on his way back to the cage. He never doubted for an instant that they would raise their rifles and threaten him if he did anything but go the way they wanted him to go.

He kept walking—as if he had a choice. He made it twenty feet before he started to feel weird. His head started to spin and his stomach turned. His vision blurred, but the prisoners didn't let him stop walking.

They kept pushing and nudging him. His legs kept moving without him even being aware of them. He couldn't feel his feet striking the ground anymore. Was he upright? He couldn't tell. It didn't seem to matter anymore.

He reeled and felt himself falling, but the next time he swam back to awareness, he was still standing up and walking across the camp. He didn't appear to have covered much distance at all. Did he fall or did it just feel that way?

Was he turning into a mindless zombie like all these other prisoners? Was this how it started?

He lurched forward a few more feet and saw the cage ahead. O'Hara, Lemon, Heckler, and Peterman all stared at him through the bars.

He stumbled once, and this time, he definitely did fall. He collapsed on one knee twenty feet from the bars. The other prisoners had to pick him up and steady him the last several paces to the bars.

The prisoners didn't stop him from leaning on the bars while the Axichis unlocked the cage. LeMaine couldn't see straight enough to walk into it, so the prisoners supported him and guided him inside.

He immediately buckled onto the floor and Lemon and Peterman surrounded him. The prisoners never once stopped holding the Hellhounds at gunpoint while the Axichis locked them all in.

LeMaine curled into a ball on the floor. He felt like he was going to be sick. He *was* sick and he lacked the strength to get up.

Someone put their hand on his forehead. It was Peterman. "He's feverish."

"What can we do?" Lemon choked.

"Nothing," Peterman replied. "We got nothing."

"We have to do something!" O'Hara murmured. "We can't let him go through with this."

"He's right," Peterman replied. "We're stuck. There's nothing we can do."

Heckler squatted down in front of LeMaine and put his face right in front of LeMaine's eyes. "Captain! What did they do? Where did they take you? Did you see anything out there?"

LeMaine tried to tell him, but the words wouldn't come. The sickness became overwhelming and LeMaine teetered in and out of consciousness even when he had his eyes open.

LeMaine couldn't fail to see the concern and even terror in all their faces, even Heckler's.

Another explosion went off somewhere.....or did it? Hecker jerked around fast and all the other Hellhounds glanced toward the bars.

"Something's happening out there," Lemon murmured. "Explosions have been going off for three days."

"I don't see anything," O'Hara remarked. "Wherever it is, it must be far away."

"It's probably nothing," Peterman replied. "The Axichis could be using these prisoners as slave labor. They could have a mine here and they're blasting rock. It doesn't help us if it's so far away."

Heckler bent down in front of LeMaine's face again. "Captain! What can you tell us about what's going on out there?"

LeMaine summoned all his willpower to get his mouth working. "The..... room....... It's........."

His brain faded out again. Peterman stripped off his jacket and laid it over LeMaine's torso. "If his fever keeps rising like this, he won't survive it."

"That makes no sense," Lemon pointed out. "The Axichis used the drug on all these people. They must have perfected it enough not to kill their subjects. What would be the point of that?"

Peterman shrugged. "I'm just saying. This is not a normal fever. A fever this high should be fatal."

The four of them turned to stare down at LeMaine. He sensed that he was letting them down as their commanding officer, especially since he didn't do anything to get himself out of this.

What should he have done—run into the prisoners' guns and let them shoot him? That wouldn't have been much help to his squad, would it?

He heard the four Hellhounds talking some more, but he couldn't make out what they were saying. They kept touching him at times, but he no longer knew which of them was doing it.

Nothing seemed real except for the time when he woke up hours later to see Peterman and Lemon sitting near him. Heckler and O'Hara were both gone.

LeMaine swam back to consciousness in the early dawn light. Only Lemon was sitting up. Heckler and O'Hara lay sprawled on the floor and Peterman was gone.

LeMaine pried his head off the floor, groaned, and tried to push himself up into a sitting position. Every limb hurt as though he'd been beaten black and blue.

He winced and squinted at Lemon trying to clear his vision. "Sergeant....."

His eyes drifted back into focus and he realized that she was sobbing silently. Tears streamed down her cheeks and her mouth twisted all the wrong way.

"Krista...." he choked and tried to crawl toward her.

At that moment, the prisoners outside rotated their weapons to their shoulders and held LeMaine and Lemon at gunpoint as Peterman staggered out of the crowd. The prisoners steered him to the bars and propped him against them while the Axichis unlocked the cage.

They pushed Peterman inside and waved Lemon out. She gave LeMaine one last desperate, devastated glance before she walked away—maybe forever.

She vanished into the crowd and LeMaine summoned every particle of his strength to crawl over to Peterman. Peterman lay crumpled on the floor, his face flushed and sweaty and his hair sticking to his forehead. He was already out cold.

LeMaine picked up the jacket Peterman had given him when he first came back from the lab. LeMaine draped it over Peterman's shoulders and went to check on Heckler and O'Hara. They both lay in a feverish stupor and didn't respond to anything he did.

He did what he could to put them in comfortable positions on the floor, but there was nothing he could do but sit back and watch. At least Lemon could cry about this. LeMaine wished he could, but he felt too crappy himself.

Even his brain felt bruised and too sore to function. He could still think clearly enough to contemplate escape. He went through all the possibilities, each one more impossible than the last.

Lemon came back a few minutes later and buckled on the floor next to Peterman. Now LeMaine was the only one left sitting up.

He kept watch all night with no change. None of the four of them moved. Were they dying? He didn't dare to check their fevers. What could he do about it anyway? No wonder they'd been so worried about him.

They still hadn't moved by the next morning when the Axichis came back for him. His mind kicked into overdrive on his way back across the camp for his second dose of the drug. He had to do something now.....but what?

The first dose had drained all his strength. He wasn't even sure he could run. He definitely wouldn't be able to fight anybody, especially not these modified prisoners who could take a carbine shot to the chest and keep on going.

Just to test out his theory, he tried to walk away from the drug room before he got there. The prisoners instantly closed around him in a tight bunch. They didn't raise their rifles or threaten. They didn't need to. They overpowered him with strength and numbers.

He did manage to get far enough off course to see the outer edge of the fence through the forest of bodies. The main gate through which the vehicle delivered the Hellhounds to this camp was the only way in or out.

Tiny silver dots flashed in the sunshine beyond the fence. They covered the ground outward from the fence line and vanished beyond LeMaine's sight. The entire surrounding thirty feet outside the fence had been mined.

Even the road beyond the main gate had been mined. Only one of those hover vehicles could get in and out. No one could set foot out there no matter who they were. Not even the prisoners could get out.

Hopeless despair overwhelmed him and he turned back toward the drug room. It really was hopeless. He was going to die out here—as close to dying as he was ever going to get while still being alive.

He didn't care about himself, but he sure wished he could save the other Hellhounds. There had to be a way.

He barely heard the explosions anymore when he stepped into the drug room. The same female technician was in there smiling kindly at him.

Commander Aga was in there, too. He smirked at LeMaine and congratulated him on finally doing something useful for the Axichis cause by becoming one of the Axichis' loyal soldiers.

LeMaine completely ignored the man's taunts. Aga meant nothing to LeMaine.

LeMaine stepped outside and another wave of sickening delirium enveloped him. He didn't remember walking back to the cage or even if he did walk there. Maybe he collapsed before that and the prisoners carried him back.

He woke up once during the following night. Deafening explosions penetrated his fevered nightmares. Were they real or did he just imagine them?

He glanced around the dark cage. The prisoners still blundered around outside it. LeMaine didn't see any explosions. He must have dreamt them.

Heckler, Lemon, O'Hara, and Peterman lay insensible on the floor next to him. LeMaine lacked the strength even to crawl to them to see if they were okay.

They weren't okay and neither was he. He couldn't hold out much longer. How many more doses of the drug would he have to take before he lost his mind completely? He hoped it would be soon.

He put his head down and shut his eyes when he heard more explosions. He opened his eyes, but he could only see darkness.

He must have passed out again because he woke up a second time. Daylight squeaked through his swollen eyelids, but his vision refused to focus.

He felt someone touching him, picking him up, and carrying him away. The Axichis must be taking him for his next dose. Hopefully, it would be his last—or at least the last one he remembered.

Chapter 16

LeMaine woke up, but he had to fight to open his eyes. They seemed to be stuck together with glue.

Someone came over to him. "Wait a minute," a man's voice told him. "Lie still and I'll help you. This will be cold."

LeMaine must have been dreaming. He recognized that voice and his heart started pounding. He tried to control it. He must either be dead or hallucinating. It couldn't be.

Something cold and wet touched his face. Someone passed a cold, wet, rough cloth across LeMaine's eyes and wiped the glue out of them.

LeMaine hardly dared to open his eyes. When he did, he looked up at Buca staring down at him. "Is that better?" Buca asked.

"What are you.....? How did you.....?" LeMaine looked around him. He was in a room somewhere—a plain room built of stone.

"How did I get here? How did I find you?" Buca asked. "Sindra told us where you were. He told us all about your mission here and what you found out the Axichis were doing."

"Sindra.....so he made it....." LeMaine gulped down relief, not only that Elia was safe, but because Buca was here.....wherever this was.

"We found Nunn, Monk, and Kellogg," Buca told him. "Galo and Polasek have been evacuated to Elian space, so you don't need to worry about them."

"Thank God!" LeMaine breathed.

"We would have come for you sooner, but it took longer to find you. The Axichis hid that camp very well."

LeMaine's head snapped around fast. "The camp! You found it? What did you do?"

Buca shrugged. "We destroyed it. The Maczhi battalion attacked it, took you and the other Hellhounds, and then we destroyed the camp with everyone and everything in it."

"I bet Commander Aga wasn't in it," LeMaine grumbled.

"No, he wasn't. He's still out there somewhere."

LeMaine gulped again. "Thank you. I can't thank you enough for coming."

"We wouldn't leave you out here—not after we found out what they were doing to Elian prisoners. Command tried to order us to stay at Ziea, but we refused. We resigned from the Military to come back for you."

LeMaine couldn't get his voice working. He didn't know what to say. "Ziea.....?"

"Don't worry. The battalion is still defending the planet, but we've declared our sovereignty from the Elian community....at least until the war is over and we can renegotiate whether we want to be a part of it."

"Why?" LeMaine asked. "Why did you leave when everything was going so well?"

"The Military refused to rescue you....and they forbade us to rescue you. They said we had to obey Command as long as we belonged to the Elian community. So we left it. We don't take orders from anyone who would send the Hellhounds behind enemy lines and then abandon them there. The Hellhounds brought back information that could save the entire Elian system. Elia owes you something for that alone—not to mention everything else you've done in your career."

LeMaine clamped his eyes shut, too overwhelmed to say anything.

Buca gripped his shoulder tight. "Stay here and rest. I have to go get Kellogg. He wanted me to tell him the minute you woke up."

Buca walked out of the room and left LeMaine alone with all these conflicting feelings. He'd been prepared to die for Elia. He didn't expect anyone to come and get him—especially not like this.

He tried to take his mind off everything that happened by looking around again. A large window in the wall opposite his bed gave a view over some mountains. He couldn't tell what mountains they were, but Buca kept talking about, 'here'. LeMaine, the Hellhounds, and the Maczhi must still be inside Axichis space.

LeMaine still lacked the strength even to sit up, but his mind felt much clearer. He could think now and his brain and body didn't feel so bruised and aching.

Buca came back a second later with Kellogg. "Oh, thank God you're all right!" Kellogg exclaimed. "We've all been worried sick about you."

"How are the others?" LeMaine asked. "Are they okay?"

"They're fine. They had fewer doses of the drug, so they're recovering quicker than you are." Kellogg pulled up Buca's chair and aimed his scanner at LeMaine's head. "How is everything working upstairs? Can you think all right now?"

"I seem to be. I feel fine except that I'm too weak to move."

Kellogg nodded and scanned the rest of his body. "That's normal. The other four are going through the same thing, though it isn't as bad for them. You'll recover."

"How are Galo and Polasek?"

"They're fine, too. They're in a field hospital on Zukion."

"Where are Sindra and Tavon?" LeMaine asked. "Are they here, too? I want to see them."

"Sorry," Kellogg replied. "They've been recalled back to the Imoliv defensive line. They were called to report to Sehiri. No one has heard from either of them since."

LeMaine sighed. "I guess I should have expected that."

Kellogg stood up. "Now listen to me. You're under orders to stay in bed until you regain your strength. The battalion is running campaigns around the countryside checking on every other place where the Axichis are keeping human prisoners. We'll be here for a few more days at least. If I hear that you're out of bed before you fully recover, I'll have no choice but to evacuate you back to Elia, too. Don't make me do that."

"Yes, Sir," LeMaine replied.

Kellogg grinned and squeezed his arm. "It's good to have you back with us."

He left the room and Buca sat back down in his chair. He relaxed like he planned to stay here forever. "Don't you have a campaign to run, Corporal?" LeMaine asked.

Buca cracked one of his rare smiles. "I'm not a corporal anymore. I'm not in the military at all now. I'm just a civilian."

"You'll never be that," LeMaine replied.

"Anyway, I can run the campaign well enough from here. People come in here, report to me, and take my orders out there. I'm a spider in the middle of my web."

LeMaine laughed. His body felt strange.

"I don't think Kellogg would appreciate you asking about the campaign, either," Buca went on. "You're supposed to be putting your brain back together, not getting all up in my business."

LeMaine cocked his head to study Buca. "So what's going on with the campaign? What are you doing on this planet?"

Buca grinned again. "I'll tell you as long as you don't rat me out to Kellogg for telling you."

"Deal."

"We've been tracking human life signs, checking on the prisoners, and then ending their lives as quickly and suddenly as possible. That's all we can do....which makes it an even better thing that we don't belong to the Elian Military. Command would never approve of that."

"You're right," LeMaine replied.

"Nunn insisted we do it that way. She said we couldn't leave even one Elian prisoner alive. She said we couldn't take them back to Elia, either. She said they wouldn't want that. She said they would want to fall here—where they died—and I guess she's right. I wouldn't want anyone taking me back to Elia like that."

"Yeah," LeMaine muttered. "Me, neither."

"We also calibrated our scanners to detect the chemical signature for the drug wherever the Axichis might be hiding it. We've been tracking down all their stores of it....and there are a lot of them."

"I'll bet there are. Have you located the manufacturing sites?"

"Not all of them. There are several on different planets. The Axichis have really been going all out to develop and mass-produce this drug. They've just been waiting for the right time to deploy it."

LeMaine shivered. "Thank goodness we found out about it in time."

"You took one for the team on this mission, Captain. I think it's only fair that you help us track down Aga. That's why you're here. Some of the Hellhounds wanted to evacuate you back to Zukion, too, but I told them you needed justice. All the prisoners did. That's why we're still here....and why you're still here."

"Thank you. I'll try not to take too long to recover."

"The sooner the better." Buca got up, clapped LeMaine on the shoulder, and left the room again.

He left a much deeper silence for LeMaine to think in. So the Maczhi battalion and Ziea in general were already declaring their sovereignty from the rest of Elia.

LeMaine suspected that would happen. He just didn't expect it to happen this quickly or for him to be the catalyst that tipped the Zieans over the edge.

He lay in bed for a long time thinking and staring at the ceiling. The sounds of activity came through the open window. Curiosity made him try to sit up. Once he did that, he found he could move more easily than he thought.

He hobbled over to the window and looked out. The building in which he'd woken up perched on a mountainside overlooking a city somewhere. Most of it appeared abandoned.

Dozens of Axichis fighters, warships, and several Elian craft dotted a field to one side. Maczhi, Cezian, and even quite a few humans worked around those craft. More Axichis fighters came in to land and Maczhi pilots disembarked, went into the city, and vanished among the buildings.

The whole place hummed with such a peaceful air that LeMaine instantly relaxed. Buca must be in charge of this whole operation. That thought gave LeMaine all the hope he needed to recover from his ordeal.

He relaxed in his room for a while, but before long, he got restless to see what was happening outside. He couldn't stay in here forever and Kellogg only said to stay in bed until LeMaine regained his strength. If he felt strong enough to walk, why shouldn't he?

He found a set of clean clothes waiting for him on a dresser across the room. They weren't his fatigues, but they would do just fine. In fact, they appeared to be Maczhi style. He could definitely get on board with that.

He got dressed and stepped out of the room. It opened directly onto a cobblestone street. All the buildings in this city had been built of stone—the same stone of which the wall of his cage had been built in the camp.

The city had a rustic, ancient feel—which explained why the Axichis had abandoned it for their newer, modern, shiny metal cities.

More voices echoed through the streets, but LeMaine didn't see anybody.

He followed the sounds and found a bunch of Maczhi, Cezians, and humans hanging out in front of another building. They didn't stop laughing and talking when he walked past them. They all seemed to be the best of friends, now that they were all fighting in the same battalion.

He wandered out to the field where all the battalion's fighter craft sat gleaming in the sunshine. They looked powerful and beautiful like this—like nothing in the world could touch them.

No one *could* touch them. The Axichis didn't dare to come after the battalion, not even here on their own planet, not when the battalion had the frequencies to defeat any Axichis vessel. The Axichis' most powerful warships couldn't defeat the battalion.

LeMaine stood there letting the fresh breeze clear his head when another squadron of fighters came screaming across the landscape from the north. A dozen craft accompanied three enormous warships burning up the mountain.

They revolved around the battalion's airfield and set down at a distance where the warships would have enough space. The pilots dismounted and Nunn and Monk climbed out of Axichis fighter craft.

They exchanged words with their Maczhi counterparts and started climbing up the hill toward the city. They didn't see LeMaine until they got near enough to recognize him.

They stopped in front of him and Monk narrowed his eyes to examine LeMaine. "Are you all right, Captain?"

"Yeah, Corporal," LeMaine murmured. "I'm fine. It sure is nice out here."

"You better not let Kellogg see you out here," Nunn warned. "He said you'd be in bed for a week at least."

"He said I could get up when I feel okay and I do." LeMaine gazed across the airfield to the countryside beyond. "I want to thank you both for staying behind. I couldn't live with myself if you went through all that."

"We should have been there," Nunn husked. "I hate that we weren't."

"You couldn't have done anything. You just would have gotten hurt, too, and there was no call for that. You both did real good staying behind to guard your comrades. I'm grateful."

She compressed her lips and nodded down at the ground. "I guess you must have heard about what's been going on around here."

"Yes, I have."

"You agree with me, don't you?" she asked. "You think I'm right....not to take anyone back.....right?"

"You would know that better than I would, Corporal—both of you would. If you say it's right, it must be. Do you agree with this way of doing things, Monk?"

"Absolutely," Monk exclaimed. "No question."

"That's all settled, then. Buca agrees with you, too, and since he's the one here making the decisions, that's the way it's going to be. You don't have to question it anymore."

"Thanks," Nunn choked.

"You did right—both of you," LeMaine went on. "We all did."

"We're going up to see the other four," Monk told him. "You should come with us."

"Okay."

They hiked the rest of the way up the mountain, back through the city streets, and into another old building. All the buildings in this city looked old, but they were all perfectly serviceable. They didn't need to be abandoned.

Nunn and Monk led the way through the halls of what looked like a hotel. The ground floor lobby opened into corridors lined with rooms.

Nunn stopped at a room with one bed in it, but the room was empty.

Voices drew the friends to a patio off the back of the building. Nunn, Monk, and LeMaine went out there to find Kellogg talking to Lemon, Peterman, O'Hara, and Heckler.

They ate and drank while they talked in normal voices. None of them was clowning around like they usually did. They all looked up when LeMaine and the last two Hellhounds stepped through the door. Only Polasek was missing.

"Hello, Captain!" Peterman greeted him.

"Are you sure you should be out of bed so soon?" Kellogg asked.

"What did I tell you?" Nunn chided. "Mother Kellogg strikes again."

"You said I should stay in bed until I regained my strength. I feel strong enough to walk around."

"What about everything else?" Kellogg asked.

"Do you want me to run the selection obstacle course?" LeMaine asked. "Maybe tomorrow."

The others laughed and LeMaine turned to the four who had been with him in the camp. "How are you folks doing?"

"We're all right," Lemon replied. "We were worried about you, but we're okay."

Nunn and Monk sat down with the others.

"Pull up a chair, Captain," Heckler told him. "Don't be a stranger."

LeMaine sat down. "If I'm a stranger, then we have a problem."

Everyone relaxed. This place was starting to feel like the Hellhounds' apartment on board Sehiri's destroyer.

"So what's next?" LeMaine asked.

"You're asking us?" Nunn asked. "You're the one who's supposed to be in charge of us, not the other way around."

"That's not what Buca tells me. He says you're spearheading the operation to go out and track down all these stashes of the drug."

"I'm spearheading the operation to go out and track down all the prisoners," she replied. "He's running everything else."

"If anyone is in charge, he is," Monk growled. "That dude is scary. He could give Command lessons in command. I have to stop myself from snapping to attention every time he walks into the room."

"He's great," LeMaine replied. "I can just imagine how they're shitting themselves back at Command now that Ziea is sovereign. The Maczhi and the Cezians in the same battalion? No one wants to mess with those people."

"Especially not the Axichis," Kellogg added. "The Elian Military and the Imoliv defense force won't have anything left to defeat once Buca finishes with them."

LeMaine looked around. "This squad doesn't feel right without the Imoliv boys around. They were real Hellhounds."

"They sure were." Heckler raised his glass. "Here's to Lutov. He gave his life in the line of duty protecting another Hellhound. May he rest in Hellhound glory forever."

Everyone else raised a glass and chimed in, "To Lutov."

They all drank and then LeMaine raised his glass. "Here's to Polasek, Sindra, Tavon, Galo, and Buca. They may not be with us, but they'll always be part of us, no matter where they are."

Everyone drank to them, too. A silence fell over the squad until Peterman raised his glass. "Here's to Mack Nunn, Edward Monk, and all the other Elians we lost in this war. May they find peace, now that they've been freed from captivity."

Everyone drank that one, too, and Nunn sniffed into her glass.

Last of all, Lemon raised her glass. "Here's to Captain LeMaine, without whom the Hellhounds wouldn't exist and we would all be dead. He was ready to lay down his life to defend Elia the way he always has. He's a true hero."

Chapter 17

LeMaine woke up the next morning to the sound of engines outside his window. He sat up and saw another squadron of Maczhi battalion fighter craft leaving the airfield.

He was just pushing the covers off when Buca walked in. "Ah, you're up. Good."

"What's going on? Is everything all right?"

"Yes, it is, but I wouldn't tell you if it wasn't. Come down to the airfield with me."

"What for?" LeMaine asked. "You're in charge here. I'm your subordinate now."

Buca snorted. "That's a good one. The Hellhounds want to come on our raids. I told them they need to check with you first."

"Why should they? You can command them as well as I can."

"They need to check with you because they're Elian Military and you're their commanding officer. I'm a civilian and the Maczhi battalion is a civilian militia. I don't have any authority to command them to do anything."

"Have you tried?" LeMaine asked. "Have you told them to go on your raids?"

Buca made a face. "Listen to you. Anyone would think you didn't want to be in charge of the Hellhounds."

"It isn't that, but if you're running these campaigns......"

"They've been on my case since they got here to let them go. I keep telling them they need your permission...."

"They have my permission," LeMaine replied. "Send them anywhere you want."

Buca scowled at him and then heaved a sigh. "Just tell them. Tell them yourself and officially transfer them to my command."

"Why so formal?" LeMaine asked. "Just take them if they're so hot to trot."

"We have to be formal because the Elian Military is involved. We need to do things according to regulations."

Now it was LeMaine's turn to make a face. "Please, son. These are the Hellhounds you're talking about. We don't do formal. You should know that by now."

"Okay, well then, *I* need to do things according to regulations. I'm going to have to deal with the Elian Military when this war is over. I don't want anyone from Command coming around saying I undermined the Military order or anything else they might say. I don't want anyone saying anything other than that I did things the right way. I still have a planet to run when this is all over."

"All right. I can appreciate that. I'll come."

LeMaine got up and Buca filled him in on all their campaigns while LeMaine got dressed.

"The Axichis are running scared," Buca informed him. "They're scrambling to defend all their supplies, now that they know we're after them."

"How is it coming with you locating all the manufacturing sites?" LeMaine asked.

"We've found and destroyed seven of them. They're scattered all over the system, so it's a project. We're assuming the Axichis must have some of the sites hidden underground or masked or something like that—something that stops us from tracking them with scanners."

"That's going to make them difficult to destroy," LeMaine remarked.

"I know. We all know. That's why the Hellhounds are so hot to go on this mission. We're already inside the system. We all want to knock out the Axichis from here so they don't invade again—or if they do, they're too weak to do much damage—or as much damage as last time."

LeMaine nodded and he and Buca left for the airfield. They kept talking on the way down there and found the Hellhounds gathered around a fighter craft Monk was working on.

Monk lay on his back tinkering with something under the landing strut. "Have you learned how to repair one of these, Corporal?" LeMaine asked him.

"I'm figuring it out with plenty of help from the Maczhi. Those boys are monsters when it comes to anything mechanical."

LeMaine glanced at Buca. "Do your boys know how to repair one of these?"

"Of course," Buca replied. "We've salvaged dozens of them from all over the Elian system. No one else was using them. We couldn't let them go to waste. Now they're in the battalion."

LeMaine bent over. "What are you working on there, Monk?"

"You don't want to know," Heckler growled.

"What about sending us out on a raid with the Maczhi, Captain?" O'Hara asked. "Buca keeps telling us to ask you."

"That's why I'm here. You're all officially transferred to Buca's command as long as we're here."

Nunn pumped her fist. "Yes!"

O'Hara thrust both his fists into the air. "Whoo! When can we go? Can we go now? Who are we hitting? What are we hitting? When are we hitting it? Please, Sweet Jesus, give us something to shoot at."

Buca raised his hands. "Wait a minute. You need to check in with Guza. He can tell you....."

"Not another commander!" Lemon snarled. "Can't you just send us out by ourselves?"

Buca raised his eyebrows. "You did not just ask me that question, Sergeant. Send you out by yourselves? Um.....no."

A few people snickered. LeMaine stood back watching and grinning. The Hellhounds were in good hands.

"So what is Guza gonna have us do?" Kellogg asked.

"You should probably ask him that," Buca replied.

The others grumbled. Heckler went over to Monk and kicked Monk's ankle. "Come on out of there, Monk. We're going to find Guza to get our orders."

Monk started to slide out from under the truss, but at that moment, for no reason LeMaine could see, the truss buckled and the fighter dropped right on top of Monk's head.

Something happened to LeMaine's implant...except that it didn't come from the implant. Without thinking, he shot out his hand and stuck it under the broken truss.

The fighter's weight fell into his hand and he flexed his arm to hold it up. He shouldn't have been able to hold up an entire Axichis fighter craft with one hand, but he didn't find the weight too difficult.

All the Hellhounds froze, especially Monk. He stared up at the fighter in stunned amazement.....and then his eyes darted over to LeMaine.

LeMaine became aware of everyone behind him staring at him with their jaws on the ground. He didn't dare to move in case he dropped the fighter, but he wasn't in any danger of doing that.

"What....the......?" Heckler growled.

"Captain?!" Nunn gasped. "What are you doing?"

LeMaine stared down at Monk's startled face. LeMaine couldn't explain what he was doing. He was standing here holding an Axichis fighter with one hand.

He didn't mean to. It happened automatically—without him even thinking about it. It happened the same way he shot those warships with the Axichis laser cannon.

Buca recovered first. "You better come out of there, Monk."

Monk gulped, blinked, and slid out from under the fighter. He scrambled to his feet, but LeMaine still couldn't move.

Buca touched his shoulder. "Put it down, Captain."

LeMaine slowly lowered the fighter to the ground. Its belly crunched on the tarmac, now that the truss no longer supported it. He didn't find this difficult at all. He could have stood there holding it up for much longer—maybe forever.

Buca stepped in front of him and LeMaine straightened up, but he couldn't stop staring down at the broken truss.

"Are you okay, Captain?" Buca asked.

LeMaine nodded, but he didn't feel okay. What the hell just happened?

Kellogg rushed over to him scanning LeMaine all over. "I guess we should have expected something like this. Didn't you say the drug made the prisoners super strong?"

"But if the captain can do something like this......?" Peterman waved at the fighter and then his eyes skimmed around the squad. "Does that mean.....all of us.....?"

"We won't know unless we test it out," Kellogg replied. "All his vitals and brainwaves are reading as normal. Everything is the same as before you took the drug—all of you. None of you is showing any adverse effects from the drug at all."

"You don't call this an adverse effect?" Heckler growled.

"It isn't adverse because it isn't putting any of you in danger. It isn't affecting your health at all. If it enhances you without impairing your mental functions, how is that a bad thing?"

Nunn patted Heckler on the shoulder. "It just means it will make you an ever bigger badass than you already are."

"Like we need that," O'Hara teased and everyone laughed—everyone except LeMaine. Did that really happen? Did he really hold up that fighter to stop it from crushing Monk?

"We need to test this out," Kellogg repeated. "We need to run you all through some obstacle course like the captain said. We need to check your strength, reflexes, agility, senses—all of it."

"How do we do that?" Peterman asked. "I'm guessing the Axichis don't have an obstacle course in this city."

"Maybe not, but I bet I can put something together." Kellogg turned to Buca. "Do you mind if I borrow one of these fighters for the rest of the day?"

"Go right ahead. Let me know if you need anything else."

Chapter 18

L eMaine stood at the end of a deserted street somewhere deep inside the abandoned city that the Maczhi battalion had chosen as its remote Axichis base.

Lemon, O'Hara, Heckler, and Peterman stood with him. Nunn, Monk, and Buca kept clear on one side of the street where they would be out of the way.

Kellogg went down the line of Hellhounds pointing out the obstacle course he'd set up. "You run down to the end of the line there, climb up the side of that building, jump over to the next building on the other side, climb down, jump on top of the fighter craft parked in the street beyond, grab the laser rifles I've left for you, and shoot at your targets."

"What targets?" Heckler growled.

"You'll see when you get over there. I'll give the signal for you to start. Whichever of you is the fastest, the strongest, and the best will be the winner. Understand?"

"Well, that will obviously be me," O'Hara added.

"The drug certainly didn't do anything to deflate your head," Lemon fired back.

"You can deflate it by beating his ass in this race," Peterman chimed in. "May the best man win."

"You got that right," Lemon snarled.

Kellogg retreated into line with Nunn, Monk, and Buca. "On your marks!"

LeMaine laughed nervously. He had no idea what to expect from this race. He certainly didn't think he could scale that building at the end of the street, but after the incident at the airfield this morning, he was starting to wonder.

What if the drug gave him super strength and super abilities just like it had given the Elian prisoners? Could it really work that fast and leave his mind intact?

Insatiable curiosity made him anxious to find out. He also experienced an overwhelming urge to beat the other Hellhounds, especially O'Hara...and Heckler. He wanted to beat them all to show he was the better soldier.

He shouldn't think like that, but he really wanted to win.

"Get set!" Kellogg called and moved his wrist in front of his face. He'd fitted his remote to the Maczhi clothes he was wearing.

O'Hara flexed his legs and Lemon crouched getting ready to spring forward. Peterman bent over and cocked one elbow back. The spirit of competition infected all of them.

"GO!!" Kellogg yelled and all five of the racers took off down the street.

LeMaine found himself skimming along the ground with no effort. He ran fast and easily. He had no trouble keeping up with the others and even glided past O'Hara.

LeMaine made it to the building first. He had no idea how he could possibly climb it, but once he got near it, his implant picked out small knobs and indentations in the rock. He never would have noticed those before. Was his implant doing this....or had his senses really become enhanced?

He jumped onto the wall without even thinking about it. He was still twenty feet away from the building when he took a flying leap and landed fifteen feet up the side of the wall.

He scrambled to the top without even straining himself. He didn't even have to look at the wall to find where to put his feet and hands. Torrents of information flooded his senses so fast he didn't have time to process it all.

He shimmied up to the roof, sprinted to the edge, and launched himself into the air without looking to see how far away the other building was.

It turned out to be way too far for any human to jump, but he soared through space so effortlessly that it didn't matter.

He landed in a crouch on the other roof and jumped off again into the clear blue yonder. He spun around and grabbed the walls.

The same thing happened. He didn't have to look to see where to put his feet and hands. He clambered down effortlessly and even looked up to laugh at the other Hellhounds trying to keep up with him. "You're getting slow in your old age, Sergeant!" LeMaine called to O'Hara.

O'Hara cursed him, but LeMaine was already pulling ahead. He spotted five fighter craft sitting on the ground forty feet below him.

He pushed himself off the wall in a Hail Mary jump and landed right on top of one of the craft. A laser rifle sat on it right between the wings.

He snatched the rifle, but at that moment, the fighter launched into the air. Its engines had been running the whole time. He heard them when he was on top of the roof, but he didn't think anything of it because Kellogg didn't mention it.

Now LeMaine realized why. Kellogg must have done this to trick the squad. He did it to test their reflexes on something they wouldn't be expecting.

The fighter rocketed into the air gaining speed and altitude. LeMaine hunkered there between the wings trying to figure out where the target was that he was supposed to shoot.

The other four craft launched behind him, and at the same instant, another five fighters took off from somewhere on the other side of the city. They screamed into view and gunned their engines hurtling straight for the Hellhounds perched on top of their own craft.

LeMaine's instincts kicked in again. He swung his rifle to his shoulder and fired without thinking twice. He didn't care which fighter he shot at. He would have targeted them all, but something in the back of his mind reminded him that this was just a test. It wasn't the real thing.

He picked out one fighter and fired a dozen times—six times into each wing. He carved off one wing and the fighter veered sharply to the right. He smashed the other wing and the fighter howled downward into the streets.

The fighter underneath him slowed and drifted down to land on the same spot from which it launched. The other four Hellhounds were still up there shooting at their targets, but LeMaine was finished. He'd won.

Kellogg rushed over with Nunn, Monk, and Buca. "That was spectacular!" Nunn gushed. "Now I want to take the drug."

"Don't even joke about that," LeMaine told her.

She beamed at him. "I'm just kidding, but it's official, Sir. You're the baddest Hellhound that ever was."

"But we already knew that, right?" LeMaine countered and made her laugh.

Kellogg scanned him again. "All your vitals are normal. Your heart rate isn't even elevated."

"I could have told you that," LeMaine replied. "I feel fine."

"You don't feel at all weak anymore?" Kellogg asked.

"No, not at all," LeMaine replied. "I feel exactly the same way I did before I took the drug."

O'Hara, Heckler, Lemon, and Peterman came over just then. "Captain LeMaine did NOT just beat all of us," Heckler growled. "That is just not right."

"We all saw him do it," Peterman replied.

"He did have an extra dose of the drug if that makes you feel any better," Kellogg pointed out.

"It doesn't," Heckler muttered.

"What does this mean, anyway?" Lemon asked. "I mean.....what's going to happen to us?"

"I'll tell you what's going to happen," Buca interjected. "We're going after the Axichis. We're going to track down every site where they're manufacturing the drug, we're going to destroy every dose of the drug, and we're going to cripple the Axichis military so they can't invade Elia again."

"Hell yeah," Monk rumbled. "Now that's a mission I can get on board with."

"Good," Buca replied. "We're gonna need all your badasses on board, now that you've all been supercharged—especially you, Captain."

Chapter 19

B uca walked the Hellhounds out to the airfield where the Maczhi battalion pilots were already loading into their fighter craft.

"What's the plan, Commander?" LeMaine asked him.

Buca pointed across the airfield. A dozen brand-new warships sat on the outskirts of the city. "The battalion captured those warships last night. They were all carrying millions of doses of the drug."

"What do you mean—you captured them?" LeMaine asked. "You destroyed them, didn't you?"

"We destroyed the doses of the drug," Buca replied. "We kept the warships. We're commandeering all these Axichis vessels for the Maczhi battalion, but we raided their log records first. We found out where all the manufacturing sites are."

"Are we going after them?" O'Hara asked. "Please say we are."

"We are. That's what we're doing here. The battalion is taking these warships to destroy the manufacturing sites. You Hellhounds are going with us in fighter craft."

"Hell yeah!" Monk cheered. "Let's ride, Hellhounds!"

"Not so fast," Buca interrupted. "I didn't finish."

"What more do we need to know?" Nunn asked. "We've been waiting a week to destroy those manufacturing sites."

Buca paused just long enough to get everyone's attention and then turned to LeMaine. "We found Aga. He's hiding in one of the underground manufacturing sites."

"The son of a bitch!" Heckler snarled.

"We're going after him," Lemon added. "To hell with the other sites. The battalion can have those."

"I thought you'd say that," Buca replied, "but you need to be careful. You Hellhounds are all juiced up, but Aga has a whole army of prisoners down there that are more juiced up than you are. We can't kill them from the air. The sites are all fortified. You'll need to go down into the tunnels and find him—and that means you'll have to fight the prisoners."

No one answered for a minute. That definitely threw a bucket of cold water on their enthusiasm. LeMaine wanted to rip Aga's head off as much as the other Hellhounds did.

Fighting an army of prisoners? That put a whole different spin on this thing.

Were the prisoners his enemies.....or were they innocent victims caught in a disaster they couldn't control? Were they collateral he should be trying to save?

Not even knowing what Nunn had been doing to them all week could change the way he felt about them. Blowing up the valley had been easy compared to this.

He didn't have to fight those people in the valley. He had just been putting them to sleep. He'd been doing them a favor by putting them out of their misery.

Facing them with guns when they were trying to kill him would be a different story. Would he be able to kill them then?

He didn't finish thinking that thought before a different image popped into his head. He saw Aga again. LeMaine saw Aga standing in that alley threatening Lemon, Peterman, and Heckler.

Aga was the one who put LeMaine and the other four Hellhounds through that ordeal at the camp. Aga was the one who turned all those prisoners into zombies and tried to do the same thing to the Hellhounds. He would have succeeded if the Maczhi hadn't stepped in and rescued the squad.

Aga. LeMaine had to kill him no matter what. LeMaine would be doing the prisoners a favor by killing them. He would be putting them out of their misery if they were defending Aga—the same man who did this to them. The prisoners would want LeMaine to do it. He already knew that.

LeMaine's vision cleared and he found himself looking at Buca.....and the rest of the Hellhounds.

"Just show us where to go," LeMaine told Buca. "We're at your command."

Buca dipped his chin. "Load up, then. Let's roll."

The Hellhounds separated, each one going to his or her own fighter craft. Buca, Guza, and their crews boarded their warships and everyone launched.

"Transmitting coordinates to your navigation systems now," Buca announced through the communications system. "The other warships will split off to go after the other manufacturing sites. We're coordinating our strike to hit all the sites at once. You Hellhounds are the only ones going underground."

"Just give us the word," LeMaine replied. "We're ready whenever you say."

"Just be careful down there," Buca replied. "We don't know what you'll find."

"We do," Peterman replied. "We'll find a whole lot of prisoners."

"And one dead man walking," Heckler growled.

Hundreds of craft streaked away from the abandoned city. Dozens of warships took off in different directions, some heading to other planets in the Axichis system.

LeMaine didn't realize until he got into the air that the abandoned city the Maczhi had been using as a base was on another planet, too—a different planet than the one where the Hellhounds had gotten captured.

The warships scattered with hundreds of fighters attending each one. They split into fighting squadrons, all with multiple species as their pilots. LeMaine had never dreamed the Maczhi battalion could get this big.

"Follow me," Buca ordered. "Aga is hiding on the fourth planet inward."

"So typical that he would have a bolt hole to hide in when the shit went down," Heckler growled.

"That will just make him easier to catch," Peterman observed.

"Heads up," Buca ordered. "We're coming into orbit. Our warships will stay in the air over your location to cover you in case anyone comes. Don't hesitate to call us in if you need air support."

"You got it," LeMaine replied. "Going down."

The Hellhounds swooped low over the planet. It was a lifeless rock with no vegetation and no atmosphere. It was uninhabited except for a few bio-domes with their own internal artificial atmospheres.

Aga's underground bolt hole was nowhere near any of those. He'd constructed it far away from anywhere people might see what he was up to—even his own people.

The Hellhounds circled the planet and four of Buca's warships stationed themselves over the bunker. A small bio-dome covered the entrance. That was the only sign that it was even here.

A few fighter craft sat parked under the dome. "Those must be his getaway vessels," Peterman remarked. "This guy thinks of everything."

"Everything except some of his would-be victims coming back for revenge," Nunn hissed. "I bet he never thought of that."

"You're right. He made sure of that."

"Until now," LeMaine replied. "We have one advantage here. He doesn't know we're coming and neither do his prisoners. Let's take advantage of it."

He lowered his fighter through the dome and landed with the other Axichis craft. His scans told him this dome contained a breathable oxygen atmosphere.

He and the Hellhounds unloaded and took out all their weaponry. Nunn packed up as much Plaostine as she could carry.

LeMaine turned to the entrance. "Now comes the interesting part."

"Did you see the scans before you unloaded?" Peterman asked.

"I didn't see anything," Monk replied. "The scans don't penetrate inside the bunker."

"That's what I mean," Peterman told him. "That must be why Aga chose this planet. The bedrock blocks scans. Whatever he's doing down there must be really important."

"All the more reason we need to stop him." LeMaine nodded toward the entrance. "Be careful down there, Hellhounds. Don't do anything risky and keep your eyes and ears open."

No one replied. They all eyed that entrance with the same flinty determination. None of them came down here to let Aga get away with whatever he planned to get away with.

LeMaine advanced to the entrance and passed his rifle across the dark opening. He couldn't see anything down there.

He switched on a light attached to his rifle barrel and it illuminated a set of concrete stairs dropping below the surface.

"So this is how it's gonna be," Lemon growled. "We're hunting a rat in his nest."

"How do we know he won't be able to escape from another exit?" O'Hara asked. "A guy who plans this well wouldn't let himself get trapped in his own bunker."

"The warships will see if he comes to the surface," Kellogg pointed out. "He can't come out without someone seeing him. That's why he's here—so no one sees him."

"Let's go, Hellhounds," LeMaine ordered. "Keep your heads screwed on straight."

He advanced down the stairs into the darkness. They ended at a flat floor thirty feet below the surface. LeMaine cast his light around a blank, concrete room with no doors or other features.

"Now what?" Nunn whispered. "This can't be the end."

LeMaine studied the walls and then had an idea. "Turn your lights off for a sec."

"What for?" Monk asked.

"Just do it for a second," LeMaine insisted. "I want to check something."

He switched off his light and then the Hellhounds did the same thing one after another. The room plunged into darkness.

Nothing happened for a second and then Lemon breathed, "Whoa!! Am I the only one seeing this?"

"No, I see it, too," Heckler murmured.

"Do you see it, too, Peterman?" LeMaine asked.

"Yes," Peterman murmured. "It's amazing."

"What are you talking about?" Nunn asked. "I don't see anything."

"The walls!!" O'Hara rasped. "I can see through the walls!"

"There are mechanical levers inside the walls," LeMaine said. "They must pivot outward somehow. That must be how we get into the tunnels."

Nunn gasped. "You can see through the walls?"

"Over here." LeMaine went to one of the walls. "This one should be it."

He lowered his rifle and placed his flat palms on the concrete wall. His eyes picked up microscopic details in the walls and beyond. He wasn't sure how, but he could see the mechanized bars and cylinders that moved the walls in and out of place.

He pushed, but nothing happened. "Help me, Heckler," LeMaine ordered. "You, too, O'Hara."

The three men took their positions in front of the same wall and they all pushed together. Then Monk helped and the wall finally pivoted on some internal axis.

The top half tilted outward and the bottom tipped inward toward the astonished Hellhounds. Once they got the wall moving, it angled by itself.

It thumped into place and locked in a horizontal position and then all the machinery LeMaine had seen made the slab drop down to the floor. It thumped into place and then sank a few more inches to form a level opening into a long, wide tunnel.

Lights dotted the ceiling running the length of the tunnel to another normal door on the far end. More doors lined the tunnel on both sides. It really did look like any normal military bunker.

"We're in!" LeMaine exclaimed. "That wasn't too hard."

"Don't ever tell anyone about this," Nunn breathed. "Don't go home and start telling people you can see through walls and shit."

O'Hara snickered. "Being a Hellhound is gonna start taking on a whole new meaning after this."

"We'll probably have to tell someone," Kellogg remarked. "We probably won't be able to keep this a secret forever."

LeMaine stopped in his tracks and turned around to stare at Lemon, Heckler, O'Hara, and Peterman. They all stared back at him as the truth sank in.

What would happen to the five of them when they got back to Elian space and the Elian Military found out about this? The Military made such a fuss about LeMaine's implant and Lemon's replacement organs.

Command would have a field day over this. They would want to test and retest and test again. God only knew how many tests they would want to run and how many obstacle courses the five Hellhounds would have to perform to show off their new skills.

LeMaine shuddered and pushed that thought out of his head. "Never mind. We have a mission to fulfill right now. We'll deal with that later."

He gave the others a chance to pull their heads together, but even LeMaine found it difficult not to think about it. What would happen to the five of them after this?

He took a step across the threshold and advanced down that long hallway. All thought of the future went out of LeMaine's head when Heckler put his hand on one of the door handles.

"Don't," Nunn warned him. "You don't know what's inside."

"I can see what's inside," Heckler replied. "There's nothing in there."

"Aga won't be up here," LeMaine interjected. "He'll be farther down and surrounded by security. We wouldn't be standing here if he was anywhere near here."

LeMaine went over to them, twisted the door handle that Heckler had just touched, and pushed the door open. The room beyond was empty.

The Hellhounds started opening the doors on both sides of the hall. They were all empty, but LeMaine and the other four Hellhounds who had received the drug could already see that.

LeMaine's eyes seemed to be doing something weird—again. He didn't understand it because it didn't feel like seeing at all. His eyes saw the walls, the doors, the floor, the ceiling—they all looked the same and as solid as ever.

Some distant part of his mind already knew what lay beyond them. It was one of the strangest sensations of his life, but at the same time, it all felt so normal and natural.

He didn't even really think of this as unusual. His rational mind registered that he shouldn't be this way, but he felt so normal that he couldn't think of himself as anything else. This was just the way he was now.

The Hellhounds stopped at the far end of the hall where the other door led to the rest of the bunker. LeMaine tried the door handle, but this one was locked.

O'Hara stood back and surveyed the door and the surrounding walls. "I can't see through these. He must have reinforced them with something."

"He knows a lot more about the drug's effects than we do," Peterman remarked. "He must have designed the drug so the prisoners could see through walls. Then Aga developed a way of blocking that sight so they wouldn't be able to see through things he didn't want them to see through."

"Being a crafty bastard won't save him from cosmic justice," Lemon countered and she raised her rifle to her shoulder. "I'll open this sucker."

LeMaine stepped away and Lemon used her laser rifle to slice through the door latch. It popped open and the Hellhounds entered another long tunnel lined with doors.

These had all been constructed of the same material. "I can't see through these, either," Heckler remarked. "Whatever he's hiding in here must be too important to him."

"Let's find out." LeMaine pointed at the other Hellhounds. "Gather around and cover the entrance."

They all raised their weapons to aim at a door while he used his laser to sever the lock. The door popped.

He pushed it open and a bellow of rage and agony came from inside. The Hellhounds stood back gaping in horror at some kind of monster inside.

Multiple limbs of different kinds sprouted from its huge, squishy body. Two tentacles, three jointed claws, and a few other different limbs from different species seemed to have been grafted onto the shapeless form.

Several eyes dotted the body in no particular order. That sound rumbled from a mouth in the center of the body.

"What.....the.....hell.......is........that?" Lemon husked.

"Aga must be experimenting on all kinds of stuff down here," Kellogg remarked.

The creature let out another roar, and this time, LeMaine couldn't help but recognize the misery and anguish in its voice. It seemed to be calling out to the Hellhounds for help.

LeMaine's insides twisted. Who knew what horrors Aga had been up to while no one was looking?

"Fire," he ordered and all the Hellhounds fired their lasers into the room.

The shots punctured the body and it burst in a gelatinous explosion of pulp and goo that splattered the walls. The creature flopped and all its many limbs slapped in the puddle of ooze on the floor.

The Hellhounds lowered their weapons as they all stared at the thing. Then LeMaine's eyes pivoted to all the other doors lining this hallway. What was behind them?

"Are we gonna do this to everything and everybody he has trapped down here?" Nunn whispered.

LeMaine glanced at her. All the other Hellhounds stared down that hall at all those doors, too. How many levels did this bunker have? It would take the Hellhounds days or even weeks or months to go through them all.

"We don't have time for this," LeMaine decided. "Come on. We got a bogey to catch."

He set off for the opposite end of the hall where the Hellhounds craved their way through another locked door.

They exited into another hall, but this one was much shorter with four elevators instead of rooms. The elevators were all Elian make, too.

"Now we're getting somewhere." LeMaine pushed the button for *Down*, but nothing happened.

A concealed screen popped up on the wall and an error message flashed on it. *Facial features not recognized.*

"Facial recognition software," O'Hara muttered. "This guy is paranoid."

"Paranoia is an irrational fear that someone is after you," Kellogg replied. "It isn't irrational to be afraid if someone really is after you."

"Forget all that." LeMaine stepped back and fired his laser into the nearest elevator.

He cut the doors apart, but when they still refused to open, he carved a giant square hole in them.

The solid steel doors tipped into the shaft and plummeted out of sight into the bunker's darkest depths.

"Let's go," LeMaine ordered.

"Where are we going, Sir?" Lemon asked.

"All the way to the bottom. Something tells me our rat likes hanging out in sewers."

LeMaine clambered through the opening he'd made. The elevator sat all the way at the bottom of the shaft. It didn't use cables or pulleys to raise and lower it. These elevators used the same engines as Axichis spacecraft. There was no way to get down there except to climb.

LeMaine's eyes picked up minute imperfections in the walls. He could climb down this easily. Lemon, Heckler, O'Hara, and Peterman could do the same thing, but Nunn, Monk, and Kellogg couldn't.

"Heckler, you're the biggest so you'll have to take Monk. Peterman, you can take Nunn and O'Hara can take Kellogg."

"Hey!" O'Hara yelled out. "Why can't I take Nunn?"

"Because I'm more attractive and that's all you care about, isn't it?" Kellogg asked, grabbed O'Hara by the chin, and planted a kiss on O'Hara's cheek before O'Hara could move or protest.

O'Hara blinked in stunned surprise for a second and then blushed. "Well, why didn't you say so to begin with?"

The others burst out laughing. "You boys could have been keeping each other warm all these years," Heckler growled. "Let's get a move on."

He groaned and belly-ached when he had to carry Monk's bulk into the shaft and climb down with him, but Heckler managed it with no problem, now that the drug had increased his strength.

The Hellhounds climbed onto the walls and started scaling their way down. LeMaine didn't have any trouble climbing. He kept looking down toward the very bottom of the shaft.

The shaft itself plummeted out of sight. He couldn't see the bottom of it. This bunker might be hundreds of levels deep. Aga had to be down there somewhere, but how could LeMaine find him?

The squad made it twenty floors before LeMaine noticed something else. The Elian-made elevator doors leading to each level didn't have the same reinforced cladding as the rest of the bunker. LeMaine could see through them.

He didn't think anything of this, either. He passed so many deserted levels that he stopped looking into them. He concentrated on what lay ahead of him—at the bottom of that shaft.

He tried to see anything below him, and when that failed, he let his thoughts drift while his body kept climbing without any help from him.

He climbed in silence for a while until, without warning, he happened to glance up. He was just passing another elevator door when he spotted a single Axichis male running away from the elevator.

"There he is!" LeMaine yanked up his rifle in a hurry. "He's right outside this door!"

All the other Hellhounds stopped climbing. "I see him!" O'Hara turned to Kellogg, who clung piggy-back to O'Hara's shoulders. "I gotta put you down......"

"No!" LeMaine countered. "Get Nunn to the bottom of the bunker. Plant your Plaostine and blow the whole bunker. That will destroy everything inside it. If Aga survives the blast, he'll have to go out on the surface where the Maczhi will capture him. Go! I'll catch him and bring him up!"

"Sir......" Monk began.

"Go, I said!" LeMaine and fired into the elevator door.

He didn't stick around to find out if they did as he ordered. He sawed through the door and sprang out into the corridor beyond. He barely caught sight of Aga running away before he darted through another door and vanished.

Chapter 20

L eMaine charged down the hall to pursue Commander Aga, but when LeMaine came to the door where Aga had disappeared, LeMaine found it locked.

He cursed Aga again and used his laser to cut through that door, too. This was taking too long.

LeMaine broke through and chased Aga through two more corridors, but Aga always gained. He could delay LeMaine by locking these doors and then sprinting ahead.

LeMaine burst through into another elevator room. Aga wasn't here. LeMaine heard the elevator moving inside the shaft. Aga was in there. Now LeMaine had him.

LeMaine used his laser to cut into the shaft and then launched himself out into the dark space beyond.

LeMaine's senses kicked into high gear. He could see more now than he could before. Being in a dangerous situation heightened his senses and all his muscles and nerves responded.

He let himself drop through the shaft. He considered grabbing onto the walls, but he changed his mind. He was falling faster than the elevator car and he landed right on top of it.

The thump of his feet on the car's roof echoed through the shaft. He really hoped that sound struck fear into Aga's heart. It was the sound of cosmic justice finally coming home for dear old Aga.

LeMaine raised his rifle and fired into the elevator roof. He didn't have any trouble balancing on it while he used both hands to carve a hole in the metal.

Without warning, another spurt of lasers punched through from below. They sliced holes in the metal around LeMaine's feet and came perilously close to hitting him.

He sprang out of the way, but the only way to avoid the lasers was to get off the falling car.

He leapt onto the shaft wall and clung there while the car plummeted out of sight. How much farther would the car fall before Aga tried to get out of it?

The lasers quit and LeMaine let go of the wall. He dropped faster and faster and all his weight slammed down on the roof. His and Aga's lasers had degraded the metal so much that LeMaine smashed right through it.

He landed on the floor and Aga lunged for him without warning. Aga grabbed LeMaine and, with supernatural strength, slammed LeMaine down on the floor.

Aga must have found a way to give himself the drug's additional strength and sensory acuity without destroying his reason.

Aga pounced on LeMaine, pinned him to the floor, and raised his fist to punch LeMaine in the head.

LeMaine reacted instantly and yanked his head out of the way. Aga's fist smashed into the floor with such force that he indented the metal.

LeMaine had to act now. He punched back, but Aga barely felt it. Aga grimaced at LeMaine in vicious hate and raised his fist to punch a second time when the car slammed into something solid.

It jolted to a stop, and before LeMaine could move, Aga sprang away, through the doors, and darted into another corridor.

LeMaine jumped up just as fast and came face to face with a whole army of Elian prisoners all gunning for him. They completely blocked the hall outside, raised their laser rifles, and fired into the elevator.

LeMaine's reflexes exploded before he had a chance to think. He vaulted off the floor and leapt through the hole that he and Aga had carved in the elevator roof.

LeMaine landed on the shaft wall again and stuck there, panting hard. He had to think. He had to find Aga and bring him down. How much longer did LeMaine have to do that before Nunn blew the bunker to kingdom come?

The prisoners flooded into the elevator, turned their lasers upward, and fired through the hole. LeMaine's brain came up with all kinds of wild scenarios for how he could get away from the prisoners, but only one made sense.

He scampered up the walls to the next level and plastered himself in place while he cut through to those doors, too. There was only one solution to this. He didn't want to do it, but he had to.

He jumped out on the next level, ran to the very farthest end of the corridor, and used his laser to cut a hole in the floor. It broke through and he jumped down to the floor beneath him.

As he suspected, all the brainless prisoners faced the elevator shaft into which LeMaine had escaped. The prisoners only cared about catching LeMaine. They were too out of their minds even to consider that he might double back and come up behind them. The drug killed their ability to think outside the box.

He hesitated there for a minute. All the prisoners had their backs to him. They were defenseless and totally innocent in this.

He hated to do it, but Aga left him no choice. All these people would die when Nunn blew the bunker. All these people were already dead. They'd been dead for years.

It still ripped his guts out to kill them, but he forced himself to raise his rifle. He wedged it into his shoulder, but he still found it impossible to shoot. These were his countrymen, his brothers-in-arms. How could he kill them in cold blood? How could he shoot them in the back?

One of them happened to catch sight of him and started to turn around. That did it. LeMaine opened fire and passed his laser back and forth across the room cutting down hundreds of Elians. Those at the front realized what was happening and turned around to return his fire, but it was too late.

He cut down every last one of them until a carpet of bodies covered the floor. They packed the elevator. The doors tried to close and failed when they bumped into bodies.

LeMaine turned away feeling sick. These were all Aga's victims. Aga killed those people, not LeMaine.

Knowing that didn't make him feel better. Nothing would ever make him feel better. He'd turned a weapon on Elian citizens. How could he live with that?

If Nunn had been here, she would have told him he did the right thing. She would have done it herself. She knew.

Thinking about her made it okay enough for him to go on. He had a job to do. Aga was still at large somewhere in this bunker. The question was where.

LeMaine cleared enough of the bodies for the elevator door to close. Then he climbed onto the roof and let the car carry him to the very bottom of the building. His instincts told him that Aga would be down there just like a rat hiding in a sewer. LeMaine had to flush him out.

The elevator stopped at the bottom of the shaft and LeMaine got out in another blank, empty corridor just like all the others. He didn't see or hear the Hellhounds anywhere. How long would it take Nunn to lay her charges? She should have done it by now.

He crossed to the nearest door. On any other level, it would have opened into another corridor of unmarked doors, each one locked and reinforced to stop anyone like LeMaine from seeing inside it.

This door didn't open into a corridor like that. It opened into a massive storehouse full of shelves rising to the towering ceiling.

Crates and crates of supplies, food, clothing, weapons, equipment, medical gear, and a thousand other things lined the shelves in orderly rows.

Most of the stuff still had the Elian Military insignia printed on the cartons. The Axichis must have been hoarding this stuff for decades.

LeMaine passed from one aisle to the next staring at everything, but this was getting him nowhere. Was Aga even down here?

LeMaine got halfway into the storehouse before he heard thumps and explosions in the distance. He followed the sound and hid behind a shelf when he found the source.

A bunch of drugged Elian prisoners manned giant Axichis laser cannons pointed at the skies. The prisoners pivoted the cannons this way and that targeting warships in orbit over the bunker.

Those warship belonged to the Maczhi battalion and they bombarded the whole bunker area, but the distant impacts didn't damage the structure at all. They couldn't penetrate this far below the surface.

The cannons spat their massive laser beams into space and the warships took a pounding, but they didn't break off.

LeMaine searched for some way to intervene and stop the lasers. There had to be some control station or something......something like the gatehouses he'd seen on Evilia.

He didn't see anything, so he took the next best option. He fired his rifle into the power coupling leading to each cannon. He severed them and brought the cannon fire to a stop.

The gunners didn't move from their seats. They sat there staring into space. They didn't even check to see what was wrong with the guns. The prisoners must have been programmed to shoot and nothing else.

LeMaine took a chance and tiptoed out onto the floor. None of the prisoners even turned around to look at him. He inched past them to search the rest of this level when he heard voices coming from beyond the cannons.

He crept forward one painstaking step at a time. Would Aga jump out and attack LeMaine here?

He stopped on the other side of the cannon station and peered into a hangar full of Axichis fighter craft. These ships looked brand new, too. They must have been part of Aga's emergency stash or maybe these were supposed to be his getaway vehicles.

The voices came from behind those fighters. LeMaine snuck behind one fighter and used it as cover to get to the next. He made his way deeper into the hangar, and as he got nearer, he definitely recognized Aga's voice.

LeMaine couldn't tell who he was talking to. LeMaine only heard one person.

LeMaine advanced to the very end of the line of fighters, stepped around it, and stopped dead.

Aga stood at a control station against the wall. He was talking to another Axichis over some communications channel, but that didn't concern LeMaine.

All the Hellhounds lay on the floor between Aga's station and where LeMaine stood. Nunn, Monk, and Heckler had all fallen facing LeMaine. He would never be able to mistake that dull, lifeless glaze over their eyes. They'd all been drugged.

His rage started to boil over. He had Aga cornered. Now LeMaine had every reason and every opportunity to put this son of a bitch in the ground forever.

LeMaine advanced and raised his laser rifle. As smart as he might be, Aga didn't see, hear, or even sense LeMaine there.

LeMaine jammed his rifle into his shoulder, took aim, and fired into the controls. They exploded in Aga's face and he lunged back, spun around, and came face to face with LeMaine's rifle pointed at him.

Aga's jaw dropped when he saw LeMaine and then Aga's startled features twisted into an evil grin. "Captain!" he sneered. "How considerate of you to join us. Your squad wasn't complete without you."

"You piece of shit bastard!" LeMaine snarled. "You deserve to die for everything you've done."

"What—you mean making you stronger and faster and smarter? I don't deserve to die for that. You'll take your new abilities back to Elia and use them against the Axichis. How is that fair?"

"You killed millions of people!" LeMaine thundered. "You kidnapped innocent people from their homes to drug them and turn them into your slaves! All those people are dead now because of you!"

Aga waved that away. "I didn't kill them. I made use of a resource to strengthen the Axichis race. Don't tell me you wouldn't have done the same thing to protect Elia."

"Protect!" LeMaine roared. "I wouldn't do that to protect anybody—and you didn't do it to protect the Axichis. You did it to conquer Elia and Imoliv. You did it to......"

A rush of vertigo hit LeMaine in the head and he reeled back on his heels. He staggered and almost fell over. He barely caught his balance in time, hauled his vision back into focus, and stared at Aga smirking at him.

"You Elians really aren't intelligent enough to rule yourselves," Aga drawled. "We realized that a long time ago. The problem was taking your natural resources without going to war against your whole Military, so we came up with the idea of forming a free-trade alliance with you first. It's a shame we didn't come up with this drug before the war broke out. We could have conquered both of your systems without firing a shot. Oh, well. Now we can."

LeMaine tried to argue back, but another wave of delirium seized him and he toppled sideways. He tried to stay upright, but he only fell onto his knees instead. He struggled to think or even to see straight.

"That's right, Captain," Aga murmured. "Take some nice deep breaths and you'll feel better. You won't feel a thing."

LeMaine looked around, but he didn't see anything to threaten him. The drug was in the air. He was breathing it in. He couldn't get away from it.

He commanded his body to stand up, but he wound up falling flat on his face instead. He fell on top of his laser rifle, which still hung from the strap over his shoulder.

The hard metal bit into his arm and body, but he hardly felt that, either. His best efforts to get up and finish off Aga only succeeded in flipping LeMaine onto his back.

He blinked up at the ceiling. He was losing consciousness fast. He had to do......something. All the Hellhounds would die here if he didn't.

He blinked one more time. Even the effort of opening and closing his eyelids took all his strength and concentration. He struggled to move any part of his body and his fingers closed on his rifle trigger grip, but he couldn't raise it. Gravity pinned his arms and legs to the floor.

Aga's face materialized directly over LeMaine's eyes. Aga peered down into LeMaine's soul, but Aga didn't sneer. He actually looked sad and maybe a little disappointed.

"Goodbye, Captain," Aga murmured. "It truly has been an exceptional pleasure knowing you. You were a worthy opponent."

LeMaine's vision blurred one more time and then wavered back into focus. Aga was still there. He didn't move as he watched LeMaine lose all focus.

LeMaine fumbled to get his mouth working. He had to say something—something important. He had to tell Aga something—something LeMaine had been waiting a long, long time to say....if he could only remember what it was.

LeMaine's mind blurred again and then, in an excruciating stab of irony, it snapped into crystal-clear focus so he understood exactly what was happening to him. He was dying. All the Hellhounds were dying and he couldn't do a thing to stop it.

Some other, mindless part of him switched on at exactly the same moment. He didn't take an instant to think before he tilted his rifle upward and fired. He didn't have the strength to lift it completely off the floor. He didn't have to.

The shot went straight through the side of Aga's head and the body collapsed right there next to LeMaine before he passed out completely.

He came around sometime later. He had no idea how long he'd been lying on the floor. None of the other Hellhounds had moved. How long had they all been lying here exposed to the drug?

LeMaine rolled onto his stomach, braced his watery arms against the floor, and dragged himself one agonizing inch after another toward Nunn. She didn't budge when he tugged her backpack off.

He ripped it open. She'd packed it to the seams with Plaostine.

He primed one of the blocks and stuck it back in with the others. That one block would ignite the others. He just had to get the Hellhounds out of here first.

His mind cleared a little more with every passing second, but his body refused to respond. If anything, he felt himself getting weaker. He had to act fast before the drug made him pass out again.

He decided to start with Monk. He was the heaviest and LeMaine didn't know how long he'd have before he lost his strength entirely.

He crawled over to Monk, grasped a fistful of Monk's jacket, and then LeMaine strained every muscle and fiber dragging Monk to one of the nearby fighter craft.

Every inch cost LeMaine an almighty effort. LeMaine couldn't drag Monk's weight up the ramp into the hatch. LeMaine had to roll Monk up it and, in some cases, push Monk with his legs.

LeMaine finally let Monk flop onto the floor in the fighter's rear compartment. Then LeMaine went back for Heckler.

Things got easier after that. None of the other Hellhounds weighed as much as those two. LeMaine had to stop several times to catch his breath and stop his head from swimming.

The job took hours—or it felt like it. He finally piled all the unconscious Hellhounds in the back of the fighter, went forward, and fired up the engines.

He used the controls to find Aga's secret underground escape chute that would eject the fighter into space. LeMaine set up a signal on the fighter's communication system in case he passed out again before the fighter got into orbit.

The message would alert the Maczhi that this fighter had human passengers on board. Buca would take care of the rest.

LeMaine crawled all the way back to Nunn's backpack lying on the floor, but when he got there, he had to stretch out on the floor and drift in and out of consciousness a few times. He was losing focus again. How much longer did he have?

He laid open the backpack, but he had trouble seeing the Plaostine anymore. He couldn't wait any longer.

He took the detonator, crawled back to the fighter, hit the controls to launch the craft, and fell to the floor when the vessel rocketed into the chute. LeMaine barely had the brain power left to press the detonator before he passed out again.

Chapter 21

LeMaine woke up in another hospital ward—an Elian one this time. The window by his bed gave him a clear view of the skies over Maenides, the Elian capital. The planets Dyson and Ar'el hovering beyond the clouds. He was home.

He glanced to his right. A long line of beds filled this side of the hospital ward. Nunn, Monk, Kellogg, Lemon, Heckler, O'Hara, and Peterman lay in those beds.

Peterman sat up reading something on an electronic device. O'Hara was sound asleep on his pillow. Nunn lay on her side with her back to LeMaine.

Monk and Heckler were talking about something and Lemon was busy cleaning a carbine.

Kellogg looked up, caught LeMaine's eye, and smiled. LeMaine tried to smile back, but his head spun again and his hand flew to his head. He felt much weaker than last time.

Just then, Polasek strolled into the ward and his eyebrows flew up when he saw LeMaine awake. "Well, look who decided to rejoin the living."

LeMaine groaned and collapsed back on his pillow. "Don't joke about that. I'm not alive."

Polasek laughed and sat down on the edge of LeMaine's bed. LeMaine tried to pretend that the rest of the Hellhounds weren't watching him and listening to the conversation.

"How are you feeling?" Polasek asked. "No, don't answer that. I don't want to know."

"No, you don't," LeMaine grumbled. "What happened? Did Buca bring us back?"

"Yeah, he did. He and the other Maczhi have been making a royal mess of the Axichis system for the last two weeks and he's been giving Command holy hell into the bargain."

"What for?" LeMaine asked. "The Maczhi aren't under the Elian Military Command anymore. They can do what they want."

"Oh, they know that. Don't you worry. They've been making it clear that everyone else better know it, too."

"What do you mean?" LeMaine asked. "What are they doing?"

"They're threatening to leave Elia unprotected if Command doesn't back off about you Hellhounds. Command wants to test you all to find out the full effects of this drug. Buca has been on their asses to leave you alone."

LeMaine looked up. "He has? Is he here?"

"No, he's back on Ziea. He says he couldn't stomach coming to the inner planets after the way Command has treated you. He's even threatened to mount a campaign to storm in here with guns blazing and take all of you back to Ziea if Command lays a finger on any of you."

"Wow!" LeMaine breathed. "He's really on a tear, isn't he?"

"You don't know the half of it. I think they would have already started experimenting on you all if they weren't so damn afraid of him. No one wants to call his bluff and I don't blame them. I've never seen him like this—except for that night when you asked him to negotiate with the Maczhi. He's furious."

LeMaine glanced over at Kellogg. Of all the Hellhounds present, Kellogg was the only one who didn't try to hide the fact that he was listening.

Kellogg returned LeMaine's gaze with that direct, no-bullshit determination of his. How much of this was Kellogg's doing, too?

LeMaine could just imagine what Kellogg had been saying to the Elian doctors about testing and experimenting on the Hellhounds.

"When can we get out of here?" LeMaine asked Polasek.

"You mean apart from you being down for the count? You're all in quarantine until the doctors determine that you aren't contagious or a risk to others."

LeMaine snorted. "You mean we're prisoners until we consent to the testing."

"Something like that," Polasek replied.

LeMaine tried again to sit up. He wasn't recovering as fast as he did last time. Would he ever? Would he ever get back to normal or had he taken too many doses of the drug?

Lemon, Heckler, O'Hara, and Peterman looked normal. Nunn, Monk, and Kellogg didn't look any the worse for wear. They'd all been awake and going about their normal business while LeMaine had remained unconscious longer than any of the others. He'd taken more of the drug than they had.

Polasek stood up and squeezed LeMaine's lower leg. "You better get some sleep, Sir. Get your strength back. You wouldn't want Command to retire you because of this."

He went over to talk to Peterman and LeMaine sank back into the mattress. He'd never felt weaker and more rotten in his life.

He didn't have any trouble falling asleep again, and when he woke up, it was the middle of the night. All the other Hellhounds were asleep in bed.

He sat up with no problem now. He still felt weak, but he didn't have any trouble standing up and walking into the bathroom.

He splashed water on his face, drank some, and walked back to the ward to find Kellogg on his feet coming toward him. "Are you okay?" Kellogg whispered. "How are you feeling?"

LeMaine shrugged. "Still weak, but pretty much okay."

"You recovered so fast the last time." Kellogg glanced around. "I wish I had a scanner on me, but the hospital staff won't let me do anything work-related."

LeMaine made a face. "This better not turn into a regular thing. I might have to crack some heads."

Kellogg smirked. "I think Buca is already doing enough of that for everyone."

"Have you been keeping track of what he's doing?"

"Only from what Polasek tells us. Command won't tell us anything. They're trying to keep us in the dark about the Maczhi battalion's campaign against the Axichis. Command doesn't want anyone to know the Maczhi are out there doing the Military's job of gutting the Axichis' next invasion attempt."

"I'll bet they don't. The Maczhi were kicking the Axichis' asses the last time I checked."

"It's worse now. The Axichis have pretty much no military left at all. The Maczhi have stolen nearly every serviceable warship and fighter craft and destroyed every base inside Axichis space. The Axichis system has become an absolute demolition zone."

"Man!" LeMaine eased back down on his bed. "I would have liked to see that."

"Yeah, me, too, but we were all stuck in here." Kellogg sat down on LeMaine's bed, too. "Unfortunately, we won't know how this added dose of the drug has affected you until you get out of here."

"How are you doing?" LeMaine asked. "How are you feeling?"

"I feel fine," Kellogg replied. "I've probably had the smallest dose out of the whole squad."

"What makes you say that?" LeMaine asked.

"Because Nunn and Monk were already out cold by the time I found them. They went into the storehouse to lay Nunn's charges. I stood guard outside to cover them in case anyone came. No one did, and after a while, when they didn't come back, I went looking for them. I found them and the rest of the Hellhounds passed out on the floor and then

I passed out. They'd already been drugged by the time I got there. I was the last one in before you."

LeMaine looked away. "I'm sorry. I should have realized Aga would try something like that. I shouldn't have sent you all into danger."

"Hey! Don't talk like that," Kellogg fired back. "We're Hellhounds. Going into danger is what we do. We wouldn't be Hellhounds if we didn't. We all wanted to go after Aga and we all knew the risks. Besides, we all made it out and we have you to thank for that."

LeMaine couldn't look at him. "Thanks."

"Thank *you*," Kellogg insisted. "You saved my life and it isn't the first time. You saved all of us. This is why you're the best commander for us. Everybody says so. Now go back to sleep. That's an order."

Kellogg chuckled at his own joke and went back to his own bed. LeMaine couldn't help chuckling, too. Taking orders from his own medic had always been something of a joke between him and Kellogg—except when it wasn't.

When the shit went down, LeMaine was more than happy to let Kellogg tell him what to do. LeMaine was downright grateful to Kellogg for taking over then.

LeMaine stretched out again, fell asleep, and woke up the next morning feeling normal. His weakness had disappeared overnight.

"Hey, Captain!" O'Hara called over after breakfast. "How about a wrestling match?"

"I'd break your arm, Sergeant," LeMaine replied. "Let's save the shows of super-manly strength for the obstacle course."

"Does that mean we're going to let the doctors and scientists test us?" Monk asked.

LeMaine looked up from the book he was reading. All the Hellhounds stared back at him listening for his answer.

"Here's what I say," LeMaine replied. "I say we give them one scan of each of our bodies, one blood sample each, and one run through the obstacle course or whatever physical agility test they want to set up. That should be enough to satisfy them. If the doctors clear us for active duty, that should be good enough for Command. That's what I'm going to do. The rest of you are grownups. You can make your own decisions about what you consent to and what you don't."

"That sounds good to me," Heckler growled. "If that doesn't satisfy them, nothing will. They might keep testing us and testing us until the end of time. We could be locked up like rats in a lab for the rest of our lives."

"Exactly—or they might decide they needed to use our blood to remanufacture the drug," Nunn added. "That would be disastrous."

The squad kept talking about it with everyone chiming in to add their own opinions. LeMaine tried to stay out of it. He'd said his piece. Saying more would only make it sound like he was trying to convince them to do it his way.

That might come across as an order. He had too much influence with these people as it was.

Polasek came back to visit a few hours later and told LeMaine that the Command staff wanted to debrief him at 1600. "I can't wait," LeMaine muttered.

He couldn't concentrate on his book after that. He paced up and down the ward and tried not to listen to his squad discussing what tests the doctors might want to do.

He counted down the minutes, and at 1545, Polasek came back to accompany LeMaine to the debriefing.

They walked in to find Colonel Nicholson, Commander Lodge, Captain Hurst, and the rest of the Command staff waiting for them. The Command staff occupied their places on the other side of a semicircular table.

Two chairs sat alone on this side. This meeting was shaping up to be more of an interrogation than a debrief.

"How are you feeling, Owen?" Commander Lodge began.

"I'm fine," LeMaine replied. "I already filed my report on our mission to Axichis space, so if you wanted to talk to me about that....."

"We don't want to talk to you about your report," Captain Hurst interrupted, "or anything else that happened in Axichis space. We need the Hellhounds to go on another mission—a mission inside Elian space."

LeMaine jolted upright and glanced over at Polasek. "That's a little out of order, Jimmy," LeMaine countered. "The Hellhounds haven't even been released from the hospital yet."

"This is an emergency," Colonel Nicholson replied. "It looks like there was one more splinter group of Axichis still in hiding that the Maczhi battalion didn't find out about. This splinter group just made a foray into Elian space and gained a foothold on Ziea."

LeMaine's jaw dropped. "Ziea! The battalion should have handled that. They had Ziea locked up so tight not even an Elian ship could get down there."

"That's what we thought," Commander Lodge replied. "It turns out the Axichis had a way to remotely deactivate their ships. They pulled this on the battalion and now the battalion is under the gun on their own planet."

"That makes no sense at all," Polasek interrupted. "If the Axichis had that ability, why didn't they use it during the war? They could have stopped the battalion from ever getting off the ground. The Axichis could have stopped the battalion from wreaking so much havoc inside Axichis space all this time."

"We don't fully understand it," Colonel Nicholson replied. "It appears that this splinter group had been keeping this remote deactivation ability secret even from its own military."

"Aga!" LeMaine murmured. "Aga did this."

Colonel Nicholson frowned. "Are you sure? He's dead."

"He was talking to another Axichis when I found him. Aga must have been in communication with the splinter group. It makes sense that he would keep this a secret along with all his other activities."

"None of that matters," Captain Hurst cut in. "We need you to go in, liberate the Maczhi....."

"Liberate!" LeMaine gasped. "What do you mean by that?"

Colonel Nicholson winced. "The Axichis are....well, we don't know what they're doing. We've lost contact with the battalion.....and the Cezians. The truth is we don't have contact with any Elians on Ziea at all. As far as we can tell, the Axichis hit the battalion, the Nulia Compound, and the Nanov Outpost all in one shot. We don't even know if any of the Elians on the planet are even still alive."

"We do know that the Axichis are on the planet, though," Commander Lodge added. "They're all over the place."

"They're moving equipment, supplies, ships, and cannons in from a different part of Axichis space—the part nearest Ziea," Captain Hurst went on. "They're reestablishing their base on Ziea to make another assault against Elia."

"I don't have to tell you this, Owen," Colonel Nicholson added. "You know it better than anyone, but none of us would be standing here if not for the battalion. If the Axichis really do take Ziea and we don't get it back—and the battalion back—we won't be able to stand another invasion."

"It's a hell of a lot worse than that," Polasek countered. "They have the drug now. They could release the drug on any Elian planet and enslave all our people. We have to stop them now before they get any deeper into the system."

"That's why we need the Hellhounds—the new and improved Hellhounds," Captain Hurst replied. "We don't have time to test your new abilities. You'll just have to test them in combat."

"All right," LeMaine replied. "We're going in. Can we take the *Belligerent* again?"

Colonel Nicholson smiled, but it was a strained smile. "We were going to assign you to her anyway."

Chapter 22

L eMaine zipped up his drop suit and pulled his hood over his head. Pounding wind thumped into the *Belligerent's* rear compartment.

The other Hellhounds stood together holding onto the anchor lines. They all wore their drop suits with their masks pulled over their faces.

Night blanketed Ziea. LeMaine couldn't see anything through the thick cloud. It was a perfect night for a drop.

LeMaine struggled forward to the cockpit and nudged Monk. "Time to go!" LeMaine hollered over the wind. "Set her and forget her."

Monk patted the dashboard. "Bye, baby. Be a good girl while Daddy's gone."

He set the auto-pilot, climbed out of his seat, and pulled his hood up on his way to the back. LeMaine yanked down his own mask and waved to Heckler, who stood first in line.

Heckler took a running jump out of the back and plunged out of sight followed by Lemon, Nunn, and Kellogg. O'Hara followed, then Peterman and Polasek.

LeMaine nodded to Monk, pulled down his mask, and launched himself into open space. He started to plummet toward the planet's surface burning through the atmosphere.

His suit started to heat up and he curled into a ball. He tucked his head under his arms and warmth throbbed through his suit as he dropped faster and faster.

His remote buzzed and he uncurled. He flung his arms out to both sides. The wind beat against the sails between his arms, legs, and body. He soared level with the ground until he found the drop zone.

He floated lower, whizzed over the countryside, and landed running to break his momentum. He ended up tucking and rolling the last twenty feet before he rolled up onto his feet.

He looked around. He was in the open countryside near the Nanov Outpost, but the Outpost was all dark now. He checked his remote just to make sure.

The remote didn't read any life signs in there, but that could be a mistake or a trick. Remotes didn't always work as reliably as they should on this planet.

It was still dark enough that no one could see him. He got busy stripping off his drop suit and getting his laser rifles ready. He insisted on the Hellhounds bringing laser rifles on this mission. The Hellhounds were going up against the Axichis.

Aga might have found a way to dose his co-conspirators with the drug and make them invulnerable to carbine fire. LeMaine didn't want to deal with any enemy who had that ability, not to mention any drugged Elian prisoners they might have brought with them as cannon fodder.

His remote did show him where the other Hellhounds had landed. He hustled across country and met Peterman, Polasek, Heckler, and Nunn gathered in the darkness. "All set?" LeMaine asked.

"Yep," Heckler replied. "There are Maczhi life signs reading at the Nulia Compound."

"That makes sense," Peterman replied. "Buca was always doing business there."

"Let's go see," LeMaine ordered. "If Buca is there, we can pay him a visit and see what's happening. If the Axichis are holding Maczhi prisoners, we can pay them a visit instead."

He tracked down the rest of his squad and they set off overland toward the Nulia Compound. LeMaine studied his remote on the way.

Plenty of Maczhi life signs were still reading in the mountains at the battalion's main camp. LeMaine didn't see any Axichis life signs near there.

He frowned at his readings while he walked. "What's wrong, Sir?" O'Hara asked. "Did your breakfast come back for seconds?"

Nunn snorted. LeMaine ignored them. "There are no Axichis life signs reading anywhere on this planet. This isn't looking good."

"That's going to make them difficult to find," Polasek remarked.

"Something tells me they won't be difficult to find at all," Heckler muttered. "We won't be able to stop tripping over them."

The squad walked for the rest of the night and most of the following day before they got near enough to the Nulia Compound for it to come up on LeMaine's remote. "Still no sign of Axichis."

"There are plenty of Axichis spacecraft, though," Lemon pointed out.

"They could belong to the battalion," Kellogg pointed out. "We won't be able to tell them apart."

"The good news is that the Axichis won't be able to tell them apart, either," LeMaine chimed in.

"How does that help us?" Peterman asked.

"We couldn't tell which fighters belonged to the Axichis and which were Maczhi except by reading the pilots' life signs—which means the Axichis can't do it, either. They won't be able to tell at all with all those fighters on the ground."

Some of the others frowned at him, but LeMaine let it drop. He wasn't sure how that helped them or if it helped them at all, but it was better than nothing.

His remote read a lot more Axichis spacecraft as the squad neared the Nulia Compound. That wasn't unusual, either. The battalion kept their spacecraft here.

They crowded the planes outside the compound, but the compound didn't read any Axichis life signs, either.

"I'm reading plenty of Maczhi and Cezians, though," Kellogg pointed out. "We need to get in there and talk to our people."

"Not if the Axichis are in there," Monk countered. "We'd get our asses handed to us."

"We wouldn't go waltzing through the front door, you mule," Lemon snapped. "Use your brain if you have one."

"Let's get closer and see," LeMaine suggested.

They crossed the last few hills and the squad hunkered down behind one of them. LeMaine flattened himself on his belly and got out his binoculars.

O'Hara raised his scope to his eye, peered through it, and immediately jolted back. "Whoa!"

"What's wrong?" LeMaine asked.

"Take a look," O'Hara replied.

LeMaine flipped over, but when he raised his glasses to look at the compound, he discovered that he didn't need them. He could see the compound perfectly well without them—and not just the compound. He could see straight through the walls at everything going on inside.

He raised his glasses to his eyes just to check and immediately put them down. He could see better without them.

He and O'Hara exchanged glances and then turned back to study the situation inside the walls. The Axichis were definitely in the house—and plenty of them.

They occupied nearly every room and held the Maczhi and Cezian residents at gunpoint. The Axichis even threatened families and children living in the compound.

"I don't see Vulo or any of the Cezian Council," Peterman remarked.

"Or any of the battalion heads, either," LeMaine added. "Where are they?"

"The Axichis probably locked everybody in the basement the way they did last time," O'Hara remarked. "Aga's crew probably knew about where the Axichis were holding the Council during their first invasion. They'll want to keep the Maczhi and the Council away from the outer walls."

"And away from prying eyes," Nunn added. "Aga probably told his people that some Elians got the drug. Maybe he wanted to warn the splinter group that some Elians had the ability to see through walls."

"That makes sense," LeMaine replied.

"We gotta get them outta there," Kellogg exclaimed. "We can't leave them as prisoners."

"Don't jump the gun," LeMaine countered. "Getting them out of there and even killing all these Axichis won't do any good."

"Of course it will do some good!" O'Hara exclaimed. "That's what we did last time. We cleared every last Axichis off the planet."

"That was last time," LeMaine argued. "We had the battalion with us last time and we also didn't have the Axichis standing by to deploy this drug over two whole solar systems. We need to use our brains like Lemon says."

"We should be using our speed and strength," Heckler growled. "Not our brains."

"Think about it," LeMaine told him. "Say we go in there with guns blazing, free the captives, and kill all those Axichis. The battalion is still grounded and none of that defeats the splinter group. It doesn't stop them from threatening our people with the drug or invasion or worse."

"So what's the answer?" Nunn asked. "What do we do?"

"We have to figure out how to release the battalion's aircraft. We need to get the battalion back in the air. Once we do that, we can stop the Axichis from using Ziea as a launchpad. We can take them from here. Command said the splinter group moved in on Ziea first, which is not what the regular Axichis military did last time. They attacked the central solar system."

"What does that mean?" O'Hara asked.

"Don't you remember, Nunn? I told Sindra and Tavon to escape at the far end of the Axichis solar system—the end closest to Ziea. The splinter group must be doing the same thing. Whoever Aga was talking to must have been hiding farther out in the Axichis system—somewhere Ziea would be the closest Elian planet to their launch point. That's why they chose Ziea. They could get across the border and strike here first before any other Elian planets could react. If we can stop them here, we can stop them from penetrating deeper into the rest of the system."

"That still doesn't help us," Monk pointed out. "We don't have any way to release the battalion."

"We don't, but I bet they do." LeMaine nodded toward the compound. "We're going in. Someone in there must know how to release those ships."

He stuffed his binoculars into his pack and started to stand up. "Hey!" Polasek yelled after him. "You can't just walk in there! They'll kill us all!"

"It's like Lemon said," LeMaine replied over his shoulder. "We can't waltz through the front door. We have to go in another way."

"What other way?" Peterman called.

"Look over there." LeMaine pointed across the landscape. He could see through the soil and even the bedrock out in the airfields.

"I don't see anything," Nunn replied.

"There are tunnels all over the place," Lemon told her.

"This place is constructed the same way as the Nanov Outpost. Whoever built Nanov must have built Nulia, too. I can see two other ways into the underground basement besides the main stairs, the same way it was at Nanov."

"How do we get to the tunnels?" Kellogg asked.

"Like this."

LeMaine strode around the compound to its other end. He didn't have to worry about the Axichis spotting him. He could see through the walls that none of them were guarding the perimeter. They hadn't posted sentries. They didn't want anyone to see them from the outside.

As far as he could see, none of the Axichis in there seemed too interested in monitoring the countryside around the compound. They were too busy keeping tabs on the residents.

The Axichis weren't using the compound's transmission array to communicate with anyone, either, not even their own system. They must have gone rogue even from their own military.

Of course, the Axichis military didn't really exist anymore. This splinter group was all that was left of the Axichis' grand imperial plans to take over the Elian and Imoliv systems, enslave their populations, and steal their natural resources for the greater Axichis glory.

LeMaine passed the walls at a safe distance and stopped far out on the planes. Several hundred Axichis spacecraft blocked anyone at the compound from seeing the Hellhounds.

He turned his laser rifle toward the ground, fired, and used it to bore a round hole into the dirt.

"How do you do it, Sir?" O'Hara breathed. "How do you come up with all the best ideas?"

"Maybe that drug scrambled my brain along with everything else." LeMaine slung his rifle over his shoulder. "Let's not waste time on that when we could be focusing on the mission."

"No, you were like this before," Heckler chimed in. "You were always coming up with these crazy hair-brained ideas."

"I guess that's why I'm in charge and you aren't. Can we change the subject now?"

LeMaine sat down on the edge of the hole, dangled his legs over the side, and dropped into one of the compound's underground tunnels. He was still almost four hundred yards from the compound itself.

The other Hellhounds jumped down and joined him. Polasek moved his hand to the end of his rifle to switch on his light.

"Don't," Lemon told him. "We can see better without it."

"Well, I can't," Polasek fired back. "I can't see shit down here."

O'Hara snorted. "It's about time we got one better on you, Lieutenant. You'll just have to go to the back of the squad with the short kids."

"I can still whoop your ass, Sergeant," Polasek snarled. "Don't give me your mouth."

O'Hara laughed, but he sure as hell didn't mouth off to Polasek again. Polasek might be smaller and brainier than his squad mates, but no one in their right mind would mess with him.

Kellogg slapped O'Hara on the shoulder in a comforting way. "Save it for Captain LeMaine. He appreciates your sense of humor better."

"By 'appreciates', I hope you mean Captain LeMaine will only whoop your ass seven times whereas Polasek will whoop it eight times," Nunn pointed out.

"Or nine....or ten....." Monk added and all the others laughed.

"Get your jollies out now, smartasses," LeMaine interrupted. "We're going inside."

A few more people snickered, but they stopped fooling around and LeMaine turned up the tunnel. Lemon was right. He could see much better without the light.

He could also see through the walls from down here. He didn't get a chance to get into these tunnels when the Maczhi battalion had liberated the Cezians from Axichis control. He hadn't even known the tunnels were here.

Now he discovered that many rooms lined these tunnels. LeMaine could see everything in them without even opening the doors.

Most contained piles of dust, dead vermin that had crawled into the rooms and died during the decades when no one had come down here, and a bunch of derelict equipment and trash the previous residents had left behind before the Cezians took over.

LeMaine halted halfway down the tunnel when his super-attuned hearing picked up Axichis voices ahead. They must be guarding the locked cell where the Axichis were holding the battalion leaders and the Cezian Council.

LeMaine tiptoed forward with his rifle raised and spotted the Axichis guards through the walls long before he got near enough to see them any other way.

Five of them stood outside the heavily fortified cell door. They talked casually about nothing related to their campaign. They must think no one could break into that cell to free the prisoners—and they were probably right.

LeMaine steered the Hellhounds back to one of the side rooms on his left, pulled everyone inside, posted Lemon and Heckler to guard the entrance, and shut the door quietly before he approached the wall closest to the cell.

He signaled the other Hellhounds and they all raised their rifles, fired into the wall, and started to carve a hole in the bedrock. It took a long time. The wall must have been ten feet thick.

The Hellhounds concentrated their fire on one small circle until a narrow crawlspace formed in the rock.

They kept working until LeMaine motioned for them to stop. He hadn't been able to see through the bedrock at first, but now the layer of stone separating him from prisoners had worn thin enough for him to see inside the cell beyond.

Buca, Zonoth, his brothers, Guza, Vulo, his brothers, and the rest of the Cezian Council and the battalion leaders all stood or sat inside. They were alone with no Axichis inside to guard them. This was a perfect situation.

LeMaine waved the Hellhounds back and he crawled into the tight gap. He worked right up to the very edge and tapped on the thin surface.

He could have broken through it easily, but he wasn't ready for that. He kept tapping at intervals and watched the reactions of the men inside.

They jumped at the sound, spun around, frowned at each other, and started talking rapidly about what might be causing the noise.

They surveyed their cell trying to see anything in the darkness. After a while, Guza put his ear to the wall and traced the sound to LeMaine's hiding place.

"Guza!" LeMaine called as quietly as he could. "It's me! It's Captain LeMaine from the Hellhounds!"

Guza jumped back in surprise. "Captain! How did you....? Where are you?"

"I'm inside the wall. Bring Buca here."

Guza had to explain the situation to Buca and the others before Buca came over. "Captain? Are you in there?" Buca asked.

"The Hellhounds are here to rescue you," LeMaine told him, "but I don't want to do it just yet. We need to figure out how the Axichis are deactivating the Maczhi battalion's ships. We need to get the battalion back in the air. It won't do any good to tip our hand to the Axichis until we have a way to defeat them."

"I know how the Axichis are deactivating the battalion's ships," Buca replied. "I could turn them back on if I could just get out of here."

"You do?" LeMaine asked. "How?"

"They have a remote transmitter attached to a new communications array the Axichis have set up at the Nanov Outpost. That's why they've left Nanov deserted—to divert attention away from the transmitter. If we get out of here, we can destroy the array and the transmitter along with it. Then the battalion will be able to fly again."

"But we'd need the battalion to destroy the array," LeMaine replied. "We can't do one without the other."

Buca didn't answer right away. "You're right, Captain. We need ships."

"Do you have any way of figuring out which ships on the planes belong to the Axichis and which belong to the battalion?" LeMaine asked. "The Axichis wouldn't ground their own vessels."

Buca hesitated again. "I'm sorry, Captain, but I can't answer that, either."

"Okay. Give me a minute and then I'll let you out. I just need to discuss this with my squad."

"Thank you for coming, Captain," Buca exclaimed.

"Command sent us. Try not to be too hard on them, Buca. They're doing the best they can."

Buca gave the wall a wry grin. "I'll try to take it easy on them as long as they take it easy on you."

"We're here, so I think your threats worked. They aren't keeping us in a lab. They need us in the field too much."

Buca turned away with another snort. "Of course they do. We're ready to act whenever you tell us to, Captain."

LeMaine scooted backward into the room where the other Hellhounds waited for him. "Did you hear all that?"

They nodded. "So how do we know which ships are Axichis and which are Maczhi?" Monk asked.

"That should be easy," Lemon replied. "We just make the Axichis think they're under attack. They'll run to their ships. Mystery solved."

The rest of the squad burst out laughing, but they made sure to do it quietly. "Good thinking, Cochise," Heckler growled. "Now if we just had a way to assault the compound without hitting any civilians...."

"We do," LeMaine replied. "Command said the Axichis brought in cannons. We just need to find them, man them with a few of you badasses, fire on the compound, and then the rest of us will gun down the Axichis that run out and try to board their ships. Simple."

More people snickered. "Yeah," Nunn scoffed. "Simple."

Chapter 23

LeMaine and the Hellhounds retreated up the tunnel and jumped back onto the planes in between all the fighter craft. LeMaine looked around in the darkness. The sky was getting lighter. The sun would rise soon.

"Now if we only knew where the Axichis stashed their cannons, we'd be all set," O'Hara remarked."

"We do know where they stashed them," Peterman replied.

O'Hara jumped and spun around. "We do?"

"Of course. They're at the Grara Outpost. It's the only other structure on the planet big enough to house them. The Axichis wouldn't put the cannons at Nanov. Buca said they wanted to make the outpost look deserted. They have to be at Grara."

"So what's the plan?" Heckler asked. "It would take us days to get to the Grara Outpost from here."

"It might have taken days before, but it won't now," LeMaine pointed out. "You could run there in a couple of hours."

Heckler's eyes fell out of their sockets. "Run?"

"Yeah....like we did during that obstacle course. You run. You're faster now." LeMaine glanced around at the other Hellhounds. "Or someone else can go if you'd rather stay here and shoot Axichis."

"Or you can shoot Axichis with the cannons," Polasek added. "I'll have to stay here since I'm too slow to keep up with you jackasses anymore."

The others laughed at him. "You can still outthink us, Lieutenant," Nunn told him.

"Damn straight," Heckler remarked. "You stay here and shoot the Axichis. Nunn, Lemon, and I will go take those cannons."

"Excellent," LeMaine replied. "Can you handle any Axichis that get in your way?"

"Oh, we'll handle them, all right."

"Once you take the cannons, just start shooting," LeMaine went on. "Don't sit around filing your nails."

"That's Lemon," Nunn teased. "She might have to get her hair done while she's at it."

Lemon hauled off and punched Nunn hard in the shoulder. Nunn howled and LeMaine stepped between them. "If you don't knock it off, I'll send someone else to take the cannons. Is that what you want?"

Both of them settled down and Heckler pulled Nunn away. "Come on. We got some miles to cover."

"Don't forget," LeMaine added. "As soon as you see fighters on the way to Nanov, turn the cannons on the outpost. Help us destroy it."

"Why not destroy the outpost with the cannons?" O'Hara asked.

"Because as soon as the cannons go off," Polasek replied, "the Axichis will run out of the Nulia Compound, get on board their fighters, and go after the cannons. We need our people here to take out the Axichis pilots and launch the battalion right away to hold the fighters off."

"You see?" Kellogg pointed at Polasek. "This is why we need you, Lieutenant. We need you to do our thinking for us."

"Isn't that what Captain LeMaine is here for?" Polasek asked.

"No," LeMaine interrupted. "That isn't what Captain LeMaine is here for. You do all the thinking you want, Lieutenant. You're so much better at it than I am." He waved the three gunners away. "Go on. Go make some noise."

They laughed and ran off into the dark. LeMaine could just imagine what kind of trouble those three would get up to in his absence.

"So typical," O'Hara muttered. "He had to take the two females with him."

"It's his funeral," Peterman replied. "I don't envy him with those two for partners."

"Everyone get into position," LeMaine ordered. "We need to be ready to shoot as soon as the cannons unload."

"Where are you going?" Peterman asked.

"I'm going to get everyone out of that cell. We need them to pilot these craft as soon as the cannons strike."

LeMaine returned to the crawlspace, used his rifle to carve the rest of the way through the thin rock layer, and motioned all the prisoners out. "Just keep quiet," he whispered. "Follow that tunnel to the surface and get outside. Conceal yourselves with the Hellhounds and get ready to launch the Axichis fighters as soon as we see which ones they are."

The Maczhi and Cezian battalion members hurried away into the dark. LeMaine stayed behind and checked on the Axichis guards. They still stood around in the same place talking and laughing. They had no idea they were guarding an empty cell now.

He retreated back outside, joined the others, and checked his remote to follow Nunn, Heckler, and Lemon as they ran across country.

"They're making better progress than I thought," Peterman remarked. "They'll be there in a few minutes."

"It might take them a while to get inside the outpost," Polasek pointed out.

LeMaine and the two lieutenants watched Heckler and Nunn skim to the Grara Outpost's righthand side. Lemon stopped fifty feet away, paused, and then walked right near the front gate.

"Damn, I wish I could see this!" O'Hara breathed. "She must be pulling the rug out from under their feet about now."

LeMaine couldn't see any Axichis on his remote, but that didn't make any difference in the end.

Lemon stayed by the front gate while Nunn and Heckler traced the outpost's outer walls. "How many is that so far?" Kellogg asked.

"Eleven blocks," Peterman replied.

O'Hara whistled through his teeth. "She just keeps going bigger and bigger with every job. When do you think she'll.....?"

A flash of light erupted on the remote as Nunn's Plaostine exploded. They disintegrated part of the outer walls and Lemon darted inside.

"And that's all she wrote," Monk murmured and leaned back to relax.

"Pay attention, Monk," Peterman told him. "The fun's just starting."

Peterman swiveled onto his knees, raised his rifle to his shoulder, aimed out into the growing dawn light, and trained his beady eyes on the Axichis fighters between the Nulia Compound and the Hellhounds' position.

The other Hellhounds did the same thing and covered the fighters nearest to the compound's entrance. "Any second now......" Polasek murmured.

At that moment, a wicked laser shot fired in the darkness to the west. It seared into the atmosphere, arced in a graceful curve, and plunged straight for the Nulia Compound. The Axichis inside were too complacent and overconfident to see it coming.

It smashed through the compound roof followed by another four laser cannon shots in rapid succession. These struck the outer walls and a few spots inside the compound, but the gunners made sure not to hit anything with people inside.

The effect came almost instantaneously. Dozens of Axichis streaked from the compound heading for their fighters. They divided with each pilot going to a different craft.

Peterman fired and then the whole squad opened up. The Axichis pilots dropped right outside their craft—the Axichis craft that the transmitter hadn't switched off.

"Go!" LeMaine yelled to the battalion leaders. "Get in the air and destroy the Nanov array! Go, go, go!"

He pushed everyone out of their hiding place. The battalion leaders and Cezian Council members charged onto the planes, kicked their dead enemies out of the way, and raced on board their craft.

Dozens of fighters launched and went screaming across the landscape. LeMaine loaded into the first fighter he came to, sprang for the cockpit, and scrambled to get his fighter in the air. No way would he miss this.

He gunned his engines to catch up with the battalion just as the cannons turned their fire on Nanov. They bombarded the outpost indiscriminately. Buildings caved all over the outpost and lasers smashed in the roof over the array.

The fighters plunged for the outpost shooting everything in sight. The Hellhounds fell in line with Maczhi pilots and ran in a continuous line over the roof protecting the repaired array.

They pounded the roof with endless shots, and as soon as they got out of the way, more cannon fire exploded from the distance, streaked into high orbit, and came down hard on the roof.

The roof collapsed and the fighters shrieked around in a deadly circle for another pass. They aimed straight and true and their shots punched into the chamber below that housed the array.

As soon as they finished and rocketed away into the atmosphere, the cannons hammered through the opening and a ground-shaking explosion went off in the underground chamber. Smoke and fire erupted through the breach as the array detonated in flames.

LeMaine pulled his fighter to a higher altitude and surveyed the damage. The rest of the fighters swooped away from the explosion and the cannons cut off.

LeMaine's scanners pinged and he looked down at the controls as hundreds more Axichis fighters launched from the mountains. Fighters and warships erupted into the atmosphere and spread out to surround Ziea. The battalion was back in business.

LeMaine started to smile when another alarm blared from the other side of the cockpit. He swiveled around and his stomach dropped when he saw another massive fleet of Axichis crossing the border from the Axichis solar system.

These came from the outer planets nearest Ziea. They swarmed into Elian space making for the inner ring. The Axichis ignored Ziea and went straight for the heart of Elia.

"Incoming!" he yelled through the communications system. "Maczhi battalion—move to intercept! Hellhounds—fall in with the battalion!"

He yanked his fighter around and dove into the swarm's path. The battalion erupted out of orbit to engage with the incoming fighters, but the battalion didn't have enough ships to stop such a huge force.

LeMaine's senses and reflexes took over. He plunged into the swarm shooting every ship on his scanners with an Axichis pilot. He didn't need to see anything else.

The swarm swallowed Hellhounds and battalion fighters. Battalion warships blasted out of Ziea's atmosphere.

LeMaine made another revolution through the horde and spotted Elian Military bombers on their way in. The Imoliv defense force closed from their side of the border. They would be here any second and the battalion held the Axichis here. The Axichis couldn't penetrate any deeper into the system.

He turned back when another alert came up on his scanners. He almost ignored it, but it kept going off until he glanced down.

His world came to a grinding halt and he couldn't tear his eyes away from the signal in front of him. More voices drifted to his ears from far away.

"What the hell is that?" Polasek whispered.

The same question kept cycling through LeMaine's brain. Something else was launching from the outer Axichis planets, but it wasn't more ships or even a single ship.

It had no life signs on board. It didn't even seem to have any internal compartment where passengers could ride.

The scanners scrambled trying to identify these new craft and came up with something that looked like thousands of tiny metal balls all stuck together into one giant mass. The thing didn't even seem to have any propulsion system.

It broke orbit and its own momentum sent it drifting on an unmistakable trajectory toward Elia. It crossed the border into Elian space, but it didn't come near the battle.

The mass drew level with Zukion and shattered as all those millions of tiny balls split apart. Their momentum didn't carry them far apart right away, but it would....eventually.

"I have a really bad feeling about this," Polasek murmured.

"What are they....?" O'Hara began when another voice cracked in LeMaine's ear.

"It's the drug!" Buca yelled from somewhere. "They're deploying the drug!"

"We gotta stop it!" LeMaine pulled out of the battle to intercept all those balls, but he didn't see how he *could* stop them all. They were already spreading to cover a wider area of space.

The instant he touched the throttle, an Axichis warship smashed his fighter from behind. He gunned the engines to outrun the warship, only to get cut off by another two warships skimming in front of him.

All the other ships from the Elian Military, the Maczhi battalion, and the Imoliv defense force were already tied up fighting the new Axichis invasion fleet. It was the perfect trap. No one could stop the capsules from reaching Elia and dispersing the drug to the whole solar system.

"We have to break away!" LeMaine hollered to anyone who might be listening. "Get out of the battle, Hellhounds—somebody! We have to stop those capsules!"

He tried one last time to split off, but the warships kept bombarding him with such force that he couldn't even turn back to defend himself.

"Stay where you are, Captain!" Buca ordered. "I'll handle this."

"What are you going to....." LeMaine glanced around searching everywhere for his friend, but LeMaine didn't see anything.

LeMaine returned the warship's fire, but he had to run for it before he bought himself a few more inches of breathing room.

He broke out on the opposite side of the battle, but a carpet of gunshots, lasers, and phase cannon fire separated him from the capsules. He couldn't reach them in time and they were already spreading too far apart anyway. No ship could stop them. There were too many. Shooting them all would take years.

Out of nowhere, a lone warship blasted from Ziea's surface with a single Maczhi life sign at the helm. The warship came from deep in the mountains and rocketed toward the cloud of capsules.

LeMaine had half a second to read its propulsion system and laser generators overloading.

"Buca—NO!!" LeMaine bellowed.

"Keep Elia safe, Captain," Buca replied and then the warship plunged into the heart of the cloud as its engines exploded.

The warship detonated and the outward rippling fireball torched the capsules to the limit of the cloud. The fire incinerated the capsules and blew the last remaining stragglers back inside Axichis space.

LeMaine stared at his controls in disbelief. That did not just happen. Buca could not have been on board that warship.

LeMaine's mind kept telling him to go back down to Ziea and talk to Buca about this, but Buca wasn't there anymore. He would never be there anymore. It didn't seem possible that he would never run through those mountains or help his people rebuild their old strength.

Screams and bellows of rage and protest broke out through the communications system coming from the Hellhounds and the Maczhi battalion. Those screams and roars expressed all the pain and grief in LeMaine's heart, but he couldn't make a sound.

He couldn't tear his eyes away from the black, empty place in space where that warship had been. LeMaine would almost rather have the cloud of capsules back than lose Buca, especially like this.

Buca had sacrificed himself to save all of Elia. Did anyone even know? Would the people of Elia even know that someone who came from such humble beginnings had done something so selfless and heroic to save their lives?

LeMaine's mind staggered when he thought of all the billions of people on all the Elian planets. They would never know the man who made their peaceful existence possible. They would never know what a treasure he had been......and now he was gone.

LeMaine didn't want to be alive in a world without Buca in it, but he had to. LeMaine had to go through the motions of finishing the battle even though it was already over.

The Imoliv deployed the frequencies and then the Elians and the Maczhi did the same thing. LeMaine spun through the battle helping the other ships clean up the last surviving Axichis.

Some warships and fighter craft tried to break across the border to take refuge inside Axichis space. The Imoliv shot forward, darted into their path, and blockaded the border so no one escaped.

The Military closed ranks and the two fleets slaughtered all the remaining Axichis. Then the Imoliv crossed into the Axichis system, found the splinter group's stronghold on the outer planets, and bombarded them to kingdom come, too. The Axichis would never threaten Elia or Imoliv ever again.

LeMaine couldn't appreciate the victory—not when it came at such a cost. He cast one last sickened glance at the spot where Buca had blown up that warship. There was nothing there. He was really, truly gone.

"Captain?" Peterman asked from somewhere.

LeMaine looked around. The Hellhounds weren't taking part in defeating the Axichis, either. Their fighters stood off to one side just sitting there.

The Maczhi had already split off from the rest of the Elian fleet to fall back to Ziea. LeMaine hated to think what things would be like in their mountain camp tonight when the warriors came back with the news.

LeMaine gulped down despair and turned away. He didn't need to see anymore. "Come on, Hellhounds. It's time to go home."

Chapter 24

The crisp, clear tones of the bugle sounded over the dress parade grounds outside the Elian Assembly, but the music gave LeMaine the chills. The summer sunshine couldn't warm the coldness in his heart and soul.

He stood at attention with the rest of the Hellhounds while dignitaries, Command staff, and officials spoke at Buca's official state funeral. They said all the right things, but their words rang hollow. None of those people had known Buca—not really.

Hundreds of Elian Military officers and personnel turned out for Buca's funeral, but it was the hundreds of Maczhi warriors standing on the nearby hillside who really mattered. They didn't approach near enough to hear the pretty speeches made by strangers.

A massive warship stood out there, too. It would have taken Buca's body home to Ziea after the Military finished this ceremony. The Maczhi would have buried Buca in the mountains where he belonged, but there was no body for them to take home and bury. He'd been completely vaporized in the explosion that killed him.

Zonoth had explained to LeMaine that his people had a tradition of returning the bodies of their dead to the planet where the dead warrior's spirit would grow and rebirth the next generation of warriors.

The Maczhi battalion had decided to take Buca's empty coffin home to Ziea instead. They'd decided to display the empty coffin as a monument to Buca's sacrifice where he could give them all the inspiration they needed to carry on their mission—the mission he started to make them as strong as they needed to be.

Zonoth, Guza, and Zonoth's brothers condescended to attend the state funeral. No other Maczhi would even come near the parade grounds.

Sehiri and several other Imoliv dignitaries attended. They'd come to Elia to negotiate with the Elian Assembly about future Elian-Imoliv relations, so they attended this, too.

Sindra, Tavon, and Galo attended and Sehiri gave permission for the three Imoliv to stand with the rest of the Hellhounds to honor Buca and Lutov, who also didn't come home from that last disastrous mission.

Three Imoliv standing on the Elian side didn't seem like much of a gesture considering that Buca had saved the Imoliv system, too, but it was better than nothing.

At last, the officers in attendance picked up the Elian flag that lay draped across the coffin, folded the flag, and gave it to Zonoth. He accepted it politely, but he barely looked at it. Did he even know what to do with it? Did he even care?

LeMaine kept staring straight in front of him through the whole funeral. He'd attended the funerals of Hellhounds who had fallen in the line of duty, but none of them had ever affected him as much as this. Buca hadn't even been a Hellhound when he died. He'd left the squad.

He *was* a Hellhound. He would always be a Hellhound. He had been the quintessential Hellhound. Nothing would ever change that.

After way too long and too many meaningless words, the officers stepped back, saluted the empty coffin, and then saluted both the Hellhounds and Zonoth's party.

LeMaine and the Hellhounds saluted back, but the Maczhi didn't. They didn't look even marginally uncomfortable that they weren't meeting everybody's social expectations.

The officers in attendance stood back and the Maczhi warriors on the hillside stepped forward. They started chanting something in their own language as they started down the hill.

Their deep, rumbling voices got louder as they drew nearer. They struck their fists against their chests and then raised their fists in the air. They lifted their voices to a shout as they all chanted together.

The Hellhounds and other dignitaries had to move back as the Maczhi surrounded the coffin. They lifted it onto their shoulders and carried it up the hill toward the warship as if Buca really had been inside.

The Maczhi chanted louder until their combined voices rose to a deafening tide of noise. It sent a shiver up LeMaine's spine. These people knew how to send off one of their fallen heroes. LeMaine thanked the stars the Maczhi were taking the coffin. Buca deserved this. He deserved all the honor they could give him.

Zonoth and his party joined the throng of Maczhi carrying the coffin up the hill and into the warship. All the Maczhi boarded with the coffin and the warship lifted off.

It towered over the funeral for a minute and then launched into the atmosphere. It vanished into space and left Elia colder, more barren, and more desolate than it had been before.

LeMaine turned back to the pedestal where the coffin had just been sitting. There was nothing there. There wasn't even a grave for anyone to visit.

"Captain?" someone asked.

LeMaine looked up and discovered Sindra and Galo standing next to him. "What's up?" LeMaine asked. "You boys are looking good, especially you, son." LeMaine clapped Galo on the shoulder.

Neither of them smiled. The three Imoliv operatives had developed the same sickened look the Hellhounds had been sporting these last few days.

"We have a favor to ask you, Sir," Sindra replied. "We'd like to join the Hellhounds—permanently—if you'll have us. I know we'd be the first Imoliv Hellhounds—the first permanent ones—but if you could see your way to accepting us, we won't let you down."

"I don't think you'll let me down, son. Does your father know you're asking me this?"

"I haven't discussed it with him. This is my decision. I don't need his permission."

"You must have some selection process, don't you?" Galo asked. "We'd be very glad to go through that to prove ourselves to you and to Command. We'll do whatever it takes."

LeMaine shot one glance toward Colonel Nicholson and Commander Lodge hobnobbing with the rest of the Command staff, the Elian Assembly members, Sehiri, and all the other bigshots.

"I don't think that will be necessary," LeMaine replied. "Buca got assigned to my command without going through selection. I could just recommend you....but there might have to be some negotiation between Command and the Imoliv fleet....which means your father, son. If he sticks his oar in....."

"I'll make sure he doesn't," Sindra cut in a little too fast.

"I'll leave that up to you. I'll ask Colonel Nicholson. As long as there are no objections from the Imoliv, I don't think it will be a problem."

Both Sindra and Galo burst into huge grins. "Thank you, Captain," Galo gushed. "I can't wait to serve under you again."

"Don't be in too big a rush. It isn't all sunshine and roses."

"Thank you, Sir, but we know what it's like." They both saluted him and walked over to where Sehiri was talking to some other Elian dignitaries.

LeMaine turned away. He tried not to notice Kellogg talking to a bunch of other Elian Command staff and medical officers.

Command had been testing the Hellhounds relentlessly for the past three days since the end of the last battle. The Hellhounds' strength, agility, sensory enhancement, and reaction time had dwindled with every passing day.

The Hellhounds had returned to their normal state. They weren't supercharged anymore, much to Polasek's delight. Now the squad was back to being just a bunch of normal badasses instead of supercharged badasses.

The Command medical staff wanted to keep testing, but when the results kept coming up normal, they had no choice but to clear the squad for duty again.

Peterman and Polasek were also up to their eyelids in conversation with people far above them in rank. LeMaine headed over to where Nunn, Monk, Heckler, and Lemon stood together.

LeMaine opened his mouth to speak when a single Axichis fighter plummeted from orbit, shrieked to a slow landing, and set down on the same hill where the Maczhi warship had taken Buca's coffin on board.

All the funeral attendees turned to stare at the ship. Then they all relaxed when the hatch opened and four Maczhi men stepped out.

Guza and Zonoth's brothers, Rolmo, Sunus, and Linau, strode down the hill and stopped in front of LeMaine and the other Hellhounds. Guza dipped his chin at LeMaine. "Captain."

"How you doing, son? I thought you and your people would go back to your mountains for good. What brings you back here so soon?"

"The four of us would like to join the Hellhounds.......if you'll have us."

"We'd love to," Heckler told him. "You're in."

"If I can get you assigned by Command," LeMaine interjected.

"How difficult will that be?" Sunus asked.

"Wait here with your new squad mates and I'll find out."

LeMaine left them standing there and went over to where Colonel Nicholson and Commander Lodge were talking to Sehiri. The three of them had broken away from the other funeral attendees so no one would be near enough to hear their conversation.

LeMaine saluted the two officers. "Sirs."

"We were just talking about you, Owen," Colonel Nicholson replied. "Come to my office at 1000 hours tomorrow morning. We have a new assignment for your squad."

"Thank you, Sir. If you don't mind, those four Maczhi over there have asked to be assigned to my squad."

"Is that a fact?" Colonel Nicholson cocked his eyebrows at Zonoth's three brothers. "I can only assume they're here with their brother's blessing. They wouldn't be here otherwise."

"I assume that, too, Sir. We'd love to have them if you approve.....and we'd love to have Sindra and Galo, too......if *you* approve, Sir." LeMaine bowed his head to Sehiri.

"My son makes his own decisions, Captain," Sehiri replied. "If you accept him and Galo and Command approves, then I wish him and you all the best in your endeavors."

"Thank you," LeMaine replied. "Your son is an outstanding soldier. Anyone would be honored to serve with him."

"So I keep hearing," Sehiri breezed.

"You only have to ask, Owen," Colonel Nicholson interjected. "Consider these six assigned to the Hellhounds effective immediately."

"Thank you, Sir. I'll see you tomorrow."

LeMaine went back to the group. Polasek, Peterman, and Kellogg had all broken off their conversations to rejoin the squad.

"What did he say?" Guza asked.

"You're in....and so are Sindra and Galo."

"The squad is gonna start looking mighty different with all these alien faces," Monk remarked.

"It's just another improvement thanks to Buca's legacy," Kellogg replied. "It was bound to happen sooner or later, but he had to be the first."

"He was a great man," Rolmo added.

"Yes, he was," LeMaine replied, "and he leaves some pretty big boots for you to fill. He leaves some pretty big boots for all of us to fill."

"So when do we start filling them?" Lemon asked.

"First thing tomorrow morning," LeMaine replied. "You new boys report to the enlisted mess at 1100 hours for your first briefing. We're going on another mission."

The End.

Keep Reading

Battalion 1 Series

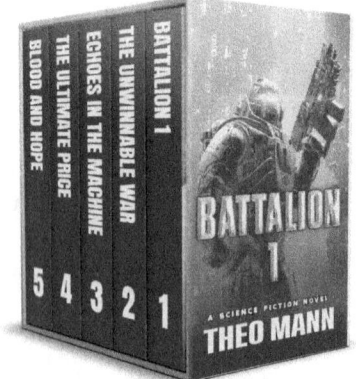

When a lab experiment goes disastrously wrong, the fate of the free world will depend on a band of broken soldiers just trying to keep what's left of their sanity in a landscape of destruction.

Captain Corban Rhodes should have died on the battlefield when a spaceship crashed on top of him. When he wakes up in the hospital fitted with robotic cybernetic implants, the consequences will leave him and those like him struggling just to survive against cataclysmic forces.

Now the fate of the galaxy rests on Battalion 1 averting a devastating alien invasion that will tap these wounded soldiers' worst fears and decide once and for all if they're still human.

You can find it at your favorite book retailer.

Sign Up Once--Get all Theo Mann's free books including brand new releases

Sign Up Once--Get all Theo Mann's free books including brand new releases

Humanity on the brink of annihilation.

A mysterious package, a corrupt officer, and a conspiracy that goes all the way to the top? What could possibly go wrong?

When a routine mission goes horribly wrong, Warrant Officer Ewing Archer and a handful of faithful friends get trapped in a battle to save the last survivors of Earth.

The human race has abandoned the ecological disaster of Earth. Now all that remains is a network of interconnected ships, stations, and satellites surrounding the planet.

But when war breaks out, Archer becomes a firebrand that could destroy it all....or save it.

Sign up at www.theomann.com to read it for free

About Theo Mann

I write 70 books per year—and yes, before you ask, all these books are my original creative work. Nothing written under my name is AI-generated or ghostwritten because I write better than AI and any ghostwriter out there.

People don't read fiction for entertainment or to escape from reality. People read fiction to see their humanity reflected in another person's character and story.

This is my promise to you. When you read my books, you'll see your own humanity reflected in the characters and stories. I take this commitment to my readers very seriously. My books are an intimate form of communication between us. I would never disrespect my readers by turning that over to a machine or another writer. This is my bond between me and you as my reader.

I write 20,000 words per day as my daily work output. If anyone with a public platform would like to challenge me to prove this in a controlled environment, feel free to contact me on this website's contact page.

I worked as a professional ghostwriter for fifteen years. Now I'm on a mission to set a Guinness World Record by writing 700 books over the next ten years and 1400 books over the next twenty years, all originally written by me. See my website for the full book list.

I'm also the author of *Proof for the Existence of God* and the *Crimes Against Fiction* blog. You can find all my nonfiction work at www.crimes-against-fiction.com.

If you have a story idea, or if you would like me to explore a series in more depth, or if you'd like me to explore a character by writing a spinoff series about that character or world, leave me a message on my website's contact page. I answer all reader emails, so ask me anything, tell me what you liked and didn't like, and let me know where you'd like your favorite series to go. I would love to hear your ideas and find out what you'd like to read next.

Find out more at www.theomann.com.

Also by Theo Mann (so far)

www.ingramcontent.com/pod-product-compliance
Lightning Source LLC
Chambersburg PA
CBHW051952060726
47506CB00011B/773